Winner Books are produced by Victor Books and are designed to entertain and instruct young readers in Christian principles. Each book has been approved by specialists in Christian education and children's literature. These books uphold the teachings and principles of the Bible.

Other Winner Books you will enjoy:
Sarah and the Magic Twenty-fifth, by Margaret Epp
Sarah and the Pelican, by Margaret Epp
Sarah and the Lost Friendship, by Margaret Epp
Sarah and the Mystery of the Hidden Boy, by Margaret Epp
Sarah and the Darnley Boys, by Margaret Epp
The Hairy Brown Angel and Other Animal Tails, edited by
    Grace Fox Anderson
The Peanut Butter Hamster and Other Animal Tails, edited by
    Grace Fox Anderson
Danger on the Alaskan Trail (three mysteries)
Gopher Hole Treasure Hunt, by Ralph Bartholomew
Daddy, Come Home, by Irene Aiken
Battle at the Blue Line, by P. C. Fredricks
Patches, by Edith Buck
The Taming of Cheetah, by Lee Roddy
Ted and the Secret Club, by Bernard Palmer
The Mystery Man of Horseshoe Bend, by Linda Boorman
The Giant Trunk Mystery, by Linda Boorman

SHARON MILLER is a free-lance writer who lives in Hastings, Michigan with her husband and three children. She owes her interest in ranching to her aunt from Scottsbluff, Nebraska who grew up on a cattle ranch there.

Sharon, who has been writing for many years, attended Evangel College in Springfield, Missouri. She has published two other books, *Danger Aboard the Evening Star* and *Tim and the Special Show Horse*, both for Moody Press.

COLBY MOVES WEST

Sharon B. Miller

illustrated by
DICK WAHL

cover illustration by
JOE VAN SEVEREN

A WINNER BOOK

VICTOR BOOKS

a division of SP Publications, Inc.
WHEATON. ILLINOIS 60187

Offices also in Fullerton, California • Whitby, Ontario, Canada • Amersham-on-the-Hill, Bucks, England

Library of Congress Catalog Card Number: 80:52902
ISBN: 0-88207-489-X

VICTOR BOOKS
A division of SP Publications, Inc.
P.O. Box 1825, Wheaton, Ill. 60187

CONTENTS

To my Aunt Belle Terrell
who made the West come alive for me
with bedtime stories of homesteading in Nebraska

1
ON THE
ROAD

There were horses, horses, and more horses as far as Colby Harris could see, stretched across the fields on both sides of the road. He moved closer to the window of the big truck that was packed with the family's belongings. Then he glanced at his father behind the wheel.

"Wow, Dad! Did you ever see so many horses at once?"

"Well now, can't say as I have," his father said slowly. "We used to have plenty to use come roundup time, but nothin' like the Mason Ranch here."

"You mean all these horses belong on one ranch?" Colby asked in disbelief.

"That's what I mean, all right. Before you've lived out here long, you'll hear the name *Mason* till it means ranchin' to you and nothing else. It's not owned by one man, but a corporation. They have the best cattle and the best quarter horses there are, some say the best in the world. I don't know of any around to top 'em."

"Wow," Colby said, letting his breath out slowly. "Is

the Two CC's Ranch anything like the Mason Ranch?"

His father chuckled and then shook his head. "I guess it's a pretty big spread by small-time standards, but no, Son. My foreman job on the Two CC's isn't any big deal. Oh, there are probably 10 regular hands, and maybe triple that come roundup time, but only several thousand acres."

"Oh." Colby stared out the window again, this time at a small herd of yearling colts racing alongside the truck in the endless dry pasture.

"Now don't get me wrong," Mr. Harris corrected quickly. "Ranchin' at the Two CC's will be everything I promised." He grinned. "You'll get your chance to learn to ride and rope, like I said."

Colby smiled back at him. The horses were thinning out now, only an occasional stray could be seen, slowly making its way to the central feeding spot near the road. Maybe the Two CC's Ranch wasn't as big or as important as the Mason Ranch. But Colby knew it must be the best there was if his dad was going to work there. His father had told him about living and working on a ranch ever since Colby could remember.

"Someday we'll go back to a ranch to live," his father had promised. At last that dream was coming true. Colby glanced in the big side mirror at the station wagon following them. He could see his mother at the wheel and Drew and Dan, the twins, in the front seat beside her. His brothers were as excited about moving west as Colby was, only they didn't really know what it was all about.

Colby hadn't minded leaving Sandsville. Well, he hadn't minded leaving the house. But he missed his best friend, Pete. And he missed Uncle David and Aunt Jo, and Mount Hope Church, and Mr. Eldon, his Sunday School teacher. . . .

"Looks like trouble up ahead."

Colby sat upright and peered down the road. A green pickup was parked on the shoulder. As their truck came closer, Colby saw a man down over the edge of the bank. The man leaned over a small horse lying on the ground, just at the side of the field. A big brown horse pranced nervously around the man and the animal on the ground.

Quickly, Colby's father pulled the truck over to the shoulder of the road and jumped out of the cab, hurrying down the slight embankment. Colby opened his door cautiously. He wanted to see what was going on too.

"Can I be of any help?" he heard his father ask.

The concerned cowhand looked up. "I'm afraid there isn't much anybody can do. I was coming back from town when I saw this here mare carryin' on like crazy. Right away I parked and hurried down to see what was goin' on. Then I found this little fellow." He pointed to the young foal on the ground in front of him.

Colby edged closer behind his father for a better look. The colt's front leg was bent at an awkward angle, and blood was pouring out of a large gash. Colby gulped and shut his eyes for a moment.

"Looks like he slipped his leg under the fence and got caught in that rusty culvert there," the young ranch hand said. "You never know what kind of a spot these curious little ones will get themselves into."

Just then the bay mare nudged her baby with her nose. The colt tried to get to his feet, but his pain was too great. He squealed in misery and fell back on his side.

For a moment, Colby felt weak and dizzy.

"Guess I might as well get it over with," the cowhand said. He stood up and started toward the green pickup. Colby watched as the man took a rifle out of the truck. He wasn't going to shoot the colt, was he? Surely something could be done for him. His leg could be set.

"You'd better get back in the truck," Colby's father said gently, putting a hand on the boy's shoulder.

"Does . . . does he have to kill him?" Colby asked. He stared down at the little brown colt.

His father nodded. "I'm afraid that's the best way."

Colby turned and ran to the truck. Though he shut his eyes and put both hands over his ears, he still heard the ringing sound of the rifle shot. He finally opened his eyes. But Colby couldn't look at the pasture. He didn't want to see the dead colt, or the worried mother horse.

His father didn't say anything as he got into the truck and started the motor. They were miles down the road before Colby could express his thoughts.

"Dad, wasn't there any other way, besides . . . besides shooting the colt?"

His father was thoughtful. "Yes . . . yes and no," he said slowly. "Trying to mend that colt's leg and care for him at the ranch, well, it just wouldn't have been worth the effort—especially for the Mason Ranch. It's very costly, and not always successful to doctor a broken leg. That colt is just one of thousands. Even if he did get well, with his bum leg, he would never be worth the time and the trouble put into him. So the easiest thing, the most practical thing, was to take care of the problem this way."

"It's not fair," Colby said tightly. He took a deep breath to help ease the choked-up feeling in his chest.

"There are a lot of things about ranch life that won't seem fair," his father said gently. "Ranching is a life of famine, drought, hailstorms, blizzards, and lots of hard work. But somehow I've always thought that the good times—working with animals, seeing a newborn calf or a baby colt come into the world and get on its feet, eating eggs and bacon cooked on an open campfire—those good times make up for the other times that are hard to take."

Colby stared out the window. He'd never thought about the things his father had just mentioned. If dealing with hard times was part of ranch life, Colby knew he'd learn to put up with them. But that didn't dissolve the hard lump in the pit of his stomach.

2
RODEO
TALK

It had been at least two hours since they had left the last Mason boundary line fence behind. Colby's stomach was finally feeling better and the lump in his throat was gone.

"There's Rio Hondo," his father said suddenly, interrupting Colby's thoughts.

Colby looked up in surprise. He leaned his freckled face out the window to stare at the small dusty village in front of them.

"It's pretty much like I remember it," his father said, parking the truck in front of the general store and looking around. "Not much here, but pure quality, all of it." He opened the truck door and looked across at Colby. "How 'bout a bottle of pop to wet your tonsils?"

"Sure thing," Colby said, opening his own door and swinging down to the ground.

"Are we here?" Drew, the tallest of the twins, asked excitedly.

"Of course we're here," Colby said impatiently, then he

grinned. "But we're not at the Two CC's Ranch where we're going to live, if that's what you mean."

"Then how come we stopped at this place?" Dan wanted to know.

"To wet your whistle, young fellow," his father said, ruffling the brown hair of the two look-alikes. "Come on, let's see what Rio Hondo has today." Mr. Harris waited until his wife got out of the car. Then he led the way across the street and into the general store.

Colby hung back. He looked all around. Rio Hondo was just like he had visualized from what his father had told him. Finally, he entered the cool, dimly lit store.

"No, it hasn't changed much in the past 50 years," the store owner was saying as Colby approached the wooden counter. "Course we paved the main street. Dust just got to be too much after a while."

"Is Old Man Parsons still banker?" Mr. Harris asked.

"Sure is," the store owner said. "Planning on needing a loan?" He smiled.

Mr. Harris shook his head. "Just knew him once awhile back."

"You folks settling in here?" the man asked.

"Yes, I'm the new foreman at the Two CC's," Mr. Harris said.

"Well, welcome," the store owner greeted. You look like mighty fine folks, ones we'll be glad to have in these parts."

Colby took the bottle of pop his father handed him and let the cool tangy liquid flow down his dusty throat.

"Got a fine school here, Son," the man was saying. "Four classrooms."

Colby tried to look politely interested. He knew a small town western school would take some getting used to. School was the last thing he wanted to think about. There'd be enough time to worry about that later.

"You'll make friends right soon enough," the store owner was saying. "Any sidekick of Cal Claypool's gets along fine right off the bat."

Sidekick? Colby glanced at his father, but he was busy helping the twins with their pop, and his mother wasn't paying attention either. She was looking over the items on the store shelves, mainly dress material.

"I guess I'll make it all right," Colby said. "Thanks."

"Well, we'd better be getting on," Mr. Harris said, placing money for the drinks on the counter. "Nice to meet you, Mr. Scott."

"Same here," the store owner said enthusiastically, holding out his hand. "Any time you're in town and I can do something for you, feel free to ask. Be glad to sell you anything you might need." He smiled broadly.

"Thank you," Mr. Harris replied with a smile. "Ready Linda?" he asked his wife.

Colby's mother glanced up. "Yes, but I'll be back for some fabric once I get settled in and have some time to sew."

They turned to leave the store, the twins racing for the door, anxious to be on the way to their new home once more. Just then the door opened and a tall, thin boy walked in, his boots clipping loudly on the plank floor. He stopped as the twins ran into him.

Colby grinned with apology.

"Howdy," the tall boy said with a smile. He nodded toward the truck. "You wouldn't be movin' into the area, would you?"

Colby nodded. "We sure are. I'm Colby Harris. We're going to be living on the Two CC's Ranch. My dad's the new foreman there."

"That so?" the boy said pleasantly. "I'm Kevin Schwartz, and I'm sure pleased to meet you."

Colby stuck out his hand to meet Kevin's while he looked the boy over. Kevin looked every bit a Westerner —from his Stetson hat to his high-heeled boots, blue jeans, and plaid shirt. Colby shrugged self-consciously. He wished he'd at least put his boots on before he'd started the trip this morning. Somehow, tennis shoes just didn't look right in Rio Hondo.

"We'd better be gettin' on," Mr. Harris said, putting a hand on Colby's shoulder. "Maybe you and this young fellow will get to know each other later on. We'll be comin' into town for church and shopping and all."

"Good," Kevin said. "Say, have you folks found a church yet? I mean, since you mentioned coming into town for services."

"That we haven't," Mr. Harris said. "You know of a good one around here?"

Kevin grinned sheepishly. "I know of the *only* church around here. My dad's the minister, but I thought you might like a personal invitation. It's just down the street around the corner to the left."

"Thank you, Kevin," Colby's mother said smiling. "I believe we'll take you up on it." She glanced up at her husband.

"Yes, we will," he said, moving to the door and opening it. "But now we really have to be going."

"Oh, one more thing," Mr. Scott, the store owner, said as he came toward them waving a yellow sheet of paper. "You all might be interested in this. Can't let you out of the store without at least tellin' you about the rodeo. Seeing as you folks are moving in and becoming one of us, let me be the first to give you the details." Mr. Scott chuckled. "Not that it'd be long before someone else filled you in. Say!" He glanced at Colby critically. "This young fellow ought to be the right age to compete in the junior division. Don't you think so, Kevin?"

"Me?" Colby knew his mouth was hanging open, but he could hardly believe his ears.

"Probably," Kevin Schwartz said nodding.

"You bet," Mr. Scott said enthusiastically. "Why I wasn't much older than you when I earned my first belt buckle, Son."

"Could I be in the rodeo, Dad? Could I?" Colby asked excitedly.

His father said, "Well, we'll see."

At last they had said good-bye to Kevin and Mr. Scott and were once again on the road headed toward the Two CC's. The dry sandy land rolled past them as the truck ate up the miles from Rio Hondo to the ranch. They hadn't passed a house or a ranch for a long time.

"We'll be home soon," Mr. Harris said encouragingly. Then after a few miles he announced, "There's the front gate."

Colby leaned forward, straining his eyes for a glimpse of the two pillars and overhead sign that were the usual signs of a ranch. There they were. He stared at the weather-beaten boards atop two fieldstone pillars. Could this be the gate for the Two CC's Ranch?

3
THE TWO CC'S RANCH

Colby's heart beat rapidly as his father parked the big lumbering truck in front of the main house of the Two CC's Ranch.

"Well, this is it," Mr. Harris said with a sigh of satisfaction, turning to look at Colby.

Just then two riders on horseback came galloping around the corner of the far barn. Racing side by side, they came to a sliding stop next to the truck. Colby could hear his mother anxiously corralling Dan and Drew back into the safety of the station wagon.

"And you are?" Colby's father wanted to know.

"Cal Claypool." The boy seemed to feel that no other explanation was necessary. "Dad's coming back in from the west pasture right now. In fact," he turned in the saddle to survey the flat pasture land, "I reckon that's his dust you see.

"Say, I forgot. Come on in the house. I'm sure Mom has something cold to drink," Cal said, putting his weight

on the left stirrup and swinging down off the horse. "Billy, be a pal and take care of Ham Bone for me, will you?"

Without waiting for an answer, Cal tossed the reins to the quiet boy on the second horse, and turned to lead the way to the ranch house. Suddenly, Colby remembered Mr. Scott, the owner of the general store in Rio Hondo. What had Mr. Scott said about Cal Claypool and his sidekicks? Was that was Billy was? Colby wondered how long it would be before Cal tried to order *him* around.

"Come in, come right on in." A smiling, middle-aged woman welcomed them into the ranch house. "We've been waiting for you folks to arrive. I've got the little house all ready. I knew you wouldn't want to take the time to clean when you were all tired from your trip here. How about a tall glass of iced lemonade? And cookies for the little ones?"

Without waiting for an answer, Mrs. Claypool took glasses down from the cupboard. "It's so nice to have another woman on the ranch again," she went on.

The cool liquid was delicious as it ran down Colby's throat. He was sure he could have eaten a dozen of the soft homemade cookies Mrs. Claypool set on the table, still in their big fat cookie jar. But a stern warning glance from his mother told him the three he had already eaten were enough.

"Want to look around?" Cal asked as Colby drained the last of the lemonade from his glass.

"Sure."

"You little guys want to come too?" Cal asked.

"You bet!" Drew said excitedly.

"Me too!" Dan answered.

The Two CC's Ranch was better than Colby had ever dreamed it would be. With Cal as their experienced guide, Colby and his brothers toured the house where they would live. Mrs. Claypool might think of it as the "little house," but it had three bedrooms and was bigger than the house they had left in Sandsville.

Next they went to the main barn where the horses being used daily were quartered. They saw the granary, the chicken house, the machine barn (a shop where repairs were done), and the brood mare barns. Here mares were brought when they were ready to foal. There were three mares with their colts in the barn. The twins couldn't stop looking at the tiny colts. Colby found it hard to enjoy their inquisitive noses, moistly poking out of the box stalls. He couldn't help but remember the little brown colt, suffering from a broken leg as a result of its curiosity, he had seen only hours ago.

It was a relief when Cal suggested they inspect the bunkhouse. Colby looked around at the neatly made bunks. The men's belongings were kept in footlockers or stashed underneath the beds. A table and chairs sat at one end of the room and a large old-fashioned wood stove in the middle. A guitar hung on the wall over the table.

"This room is used all the time," Cal explained. "That part of the bunkhouse can be opened up when we hire on extra hands for roundup." He pointed to a door at the end of the room which led to the other section of the bunkhouse.

"Have you ever stayed overnight in here?" Colby asked hesitantly.

Cal grinned. "Sure. All the time, that is, when I want to. Tom and Shorty used to bring me out here when I was littler than your brothers. Mom never really liked it when I stayed with all the men, but Dad said it would be good for me. So I got to sleep in the bunkhouse more than I did my own bed." He grinned. "Only thing, I always slept through breakfast. I'd wake up and the men would be gone. Sure used to make me mad."

"Do you think the ranch hands would let me sleep here?" Drew asked excitedly.

"Could be, Squirt," Cal said with a laugh. "You'll have to ask them yourself."

"Can we see your horse?" Dan wanted to know.

"Ol' Ham Bone?"

"He didn't seem very old to me," Colby commented. Of course he didn't know much about horses, just what his father had told him.

"You've got a good eye," Cal said, clapping Colby on the back. " 'Course it shouldn't be too difficult to see that Ham Bone is one of the best reinin' horses around. I can make him turn on a dime, or do just about anything else."

Colby nodded his head. He wanted to look like he knew just what Cal was talking about.

"You know how to ride?" Cal asked abruptly.

Colby shook his head. "Not really. I've only ridden once in my life."

Cal roared with laughter. "And you're a ranch foreman's son? Whoopee! Wait till the guys hear this. A ranch foreman's kid and you can't ride a horse!"

4
POKEY

"No kiddin', you really can't ride a horse?" Cal asked, once he caught his breath from laughing so hard.

Colby could feel his neck and face turning a deep red.

"No, I can't," he said with embarrassment. "We've always lived in town. You can't have horses there." Colby felt a need to explain. It wasn't really his father's fault that he couldn't ride, or his own either. Still, Cal was trying to make it seem that way. He felt himself getting angry.

"Man," Cal said, his face and voice serious, "we've got to do something about this problem. How about having your first riding lesson right now?"

Colby hesitated. He wasn't sure his father would approve. His dad had promised to teach him to ride, on the right horse of course. Still . . . it sounded like Cal wanted to make up for having poked so much fun at him. Colby hated to say no; besides, he didn't want to embarrass his father in front of the ranch hands.

"I . . . I guess I'd like to learn how to ride, that is, if you really want to teach me," Colby stammered.

"Nothin' to it," Cal assured him.

"I'm just not sure my dad would want me to get on a horse without . . ." He stopped. He didn't want to seem like a baby to Cal.

"Aw, your dad will be proud that you've learned how to ride a horse. He won't mind at all. Come on. Help me saddle up Pokey."

"Pokey?" Drew said, wrinkling his nose. The twins had suddenly become interested in what was happening.

"Best old horse the Two CC's has," Cal assured the twins. "He's so old he just ambles around the corral. He enjoys teaching people how to ride. You'll see."

"Would you teach us to ride?" the twins began clamoring.

Cal winked. "Tell you what. When you're ready, I'll put you two on King, the little pony in the corral outside. He's more your size."

Colby swallowed hard as the twins raced toward the corral. His stomach felt like it was full of butterflies. He took deep breaths to calm himself—but it didn't help. Cal whistled and a huge bay gelding trotted up.

"See? He's just a big baby. Here, you hold him while I get the saddle and bridle," Cal instructed.

Colby took hold of the end of the lead rope Cal had snapped onto Pokey's halter. He looked at the horse. Pokey stared back at him through sad brown eyes. He sure didn't look pokey. He was the biggest horse Colby had ever seen. Just standing next to Pokey scared Colby. He couldn't imagine riding the animal.

"How's it going?" Cal asked, coming from the tack room loaded down with a saddle, blanket, and bridle. "You two make friends yet?"

Colby shrugged, careful not to move enough to bother the horse. "I think so."

"Here, hold this," Cal directed, handing Colby the leather bridle. Cal set the saddle on the ground while he put the blanket on Pokey's back. The horse didn't even seem to notice as Cal swung the heavy saddle into place and then tightened the cinch, which went under the belly to hold the saddle firmly on. Next he buckled the back strap.

"There," Cal said taking the bridle from Colby. "We're almost ready to go."

Colby glanced toward the house. He sure wished his dad would just happen to come out on the porch. He might get into trouble, but it would sure beat having to ride a horse. Maybe the big bay horse *was* the gentlest on the ranch. But Colby still would just as soon have had his dad around for his first real ride.

"There we are," Cal said, slapping Pokey on the neck. He turned to Colby. "All set?"

"I . . . I guess I am," he said finally.

"Come on," Cal ordered, taking the reins and leading Pokey into the middle of a small corral. He slid the barn door shut on its rollers. Next he put the reins over Pokey's head and around the saddle horn.

"Up you go," he said cheerfully.

"Don't . . . don't you think you ought to ride him first?" Colby suggested, stalling for time.

"Naw. I know you're just dying to ride," Cal said generously. "I get to ride all the time. You go ahead."

Colby put his tennis shoe in the stirrup as he had seen other people do. Carefully, he hauled himself into the saddle with both hands on the saddle horn. It wasn't as easy to get into the saddle as it had looked on television.

"Put both feet in the stirrups," Cal was saying. "Keep your toes in and your heels down. You want to rest your weight on the balls of your feet."

Colby was trying to do as Cal said, but he couldn't remember half of the instructions. He felt Cal put the reins in his hands and tell Pokey to go. Slowly, Pokey started moving. Colby grinned. He was actually riding a horse! If his dad could just see him now. He relaxed in the saddle a bit. He wasn't going to fall off or make a fool of himself after all. This wasn't hard. In fact, it was fun.

Colby took his eyes off Pokey to grin at Cal. Suddenly, he saw several men leaning on the high corral fence. Where had everybody come from? What were they looking at? Him? He felt his neck start to get red. He couldn't ride well enough to have an audience, not yet anyway.

Then, before Colby knew what was happening, Pokey put his head down between his legs, pulling the reins out of Colby's hands. The horse's hooves went high in the air. Colby felt his feet fly out of the stirrups. He went into the air and landed with a thud in the dust. There he was,

staring up at the laughing faces looking at him from the top of the corral fence.

Colby tried to get up, but he couldn't move. He couldn't even speak. Or breathe. And his whole body hurt. It had been a trick—a mean, dirty trick. Cal had known that Pokey would buck him off all along.

Finally, Colby caught his breath. He moved his arms carefully. He wanted nothing more than to get out of that paddock, away from the laughter. He had fallen for a stupid ranch hand trick.

As soon as he could move, Colby got painfully to his feet. He glanced at the horse. Pokey was patiently standing on the opposite side of the corral. He didn't act like he had ever bucked off anyone. But Colby was sure that the horse was as tickled about the show that had just gone on as the ranch hands were.

"Are you OK?" Cal wanted to know as Colby limped slowly to the gate.

Colby nodded, shaking off the helping hand Cal offered.

"I guess putting people on Pokey *is* a dirty trick," Cal admitted, "but every new guy here gets the same treatment."

"Thanks a lot," Colby muttered.

"Hey, I hope you're not mad about it."

Colby shrugged. He was sore all over—and disgusted with himself.

"Well, if there's a test to belonging to the Two CC's, riding Pokey is it. And there are only a few guys who can do that. A greenie hasn't got a chance if that's any consolation. But you're all right, Colby." Cal clapped him across the shoulders once more.

Colby winced from pain and looked up into the stern face of his father.

5
FEELIN'
BAD

The hot water felt good as Colby rested his aching body against the back of the bathtub. It had hurt as much to be made a fool of in front of all the ranch hands as it had to hit that hard corral dirt. He settled deeper into the water, letting the suds come up to his chin.

As the water soothed him, Colby remembered the talk with his dad. Once his father had assured himself that Colby had not broken any bones, they had gone into the barn for a little talk—just the two of them. Colby frowned in shame at the memory.

"I suppose this little incident is as much my fault as yours, Son," Mr. Harris had begun. "I guess I've been away from ranchin' so long that I've forgotten some of the stunts that get pulled on all newcomers. But I really expected a little more sense on your part."

Colby had stared at the stable floor in misery.

"When we first talked about your learning to ride, I told you that I would select a gentle horse for your first mount." Colby nodded as his father went on. "I also told you that you should never, NEVER ride without wearing your boots."

Colby's eyes wandered across the dirt floor and back to his blue and white sneakers. His brand-new cowboy boots were still packed in the truck.

"Furthermore," his father had continued, "although we will be living on a ranch, I still expect you to ask permission before doing things—ESPECIALLY something as dangerous as riding. I know everyone thinks what just happened here was a joke, but you could have been killed. Pokey is a well-trained bronco. He loves to dump unsuspecting riders. You might have caught your foot in the stirrup and been stepped on, or dragged to your death, or ended up in the hospital with broken bones —instead of just being shaken up."

There was a long, long silence in the barn as Colby thought about what had just been said.

"I . . . I'm sorry, Sir," Colby said finally.

"Me too, Son," his dad said, putting a gentle hand on his shoulder. "We can thank God that you only ended up with a few bruises."

Colby let out a deep sigh that blew bubbles across the bath water. More than anything else, he felt sick that he had disappointed his dad. And he had broken the fifth commandment. He had learned all the Commandments in Sunday School in Sandsville. Mr. Eldon, his teacher, had said that the fifth one was probably the most difficult for someone Colby's age to obey.

Colby sighed. *Honor thy father and thy mother.* The words ran through his mind over and over. But the worst part was that even as Cal was talking him into riding Pokey, Colby had known that he shouldn't. Oh, he hadn't suspected a trick. And, his dad hadn't said that he couldn't ride—but Colby had been pretty sure that his dad wouldn't approve. If only he had followed his conscience.

The first night, the Harrises only unloaded the beds from the truck. The next day, after a big breakfast in the main ranch house, it was work time. Unloading and lugging boxes into the house was hard work. Colby's body ached from the tugging and lifting—and his ride on Pokey.

It was still a big joke on the ranch. Every time he ran into the cowhands, they asked him if he would like to learn to ride. Colby tried to be cheerful about it. But it would be nice when everyone forgot what a dope he had been.

As soon as he had a spare minute, Colby hurried up to his room. It was the best room in the house. And it was all his—he didn't have to share it with the twins. Dan and Drew were good brothers, but they could never stay out of his stuff.

He kicked off his new boots and rubbed his feet as he sat on the bed. Then he thought of Kevin Schwartz. Colby was glad that he had already met someone at the new church. Maybe Kevin could fill him in on the rodeo. Colby reached under his pillow and pulled out the yellow rodeo bill Mr. Scott had given his father.

He read through the list of events, paying special attention to the "Junior Events" section. Colby read that part of the list intently. *Calf roping. Goat tying. Doubles race.* Those all sounded like things he might be able to do—with a lot of practice. *Boot scramble.* He grinned. That event sounded like something the twins could do.

It was strange that no one on the ranch had said anything about the rodeo. Most of the talk Colby had overheard between the ranch hands had concerned mending fences, feeding stock, or caring for the range cattle. Maybe the men on the Two CC's didn't go in to Rio Hondo for the rodeo. But Colby's father had said that *everyone* would go to the rodeo. It just didn't make sense.

"Colby?" his mother called from the living room.

Colby answered, hurrying down the stairs.

"Drew and Dan have wandered off again," his mother said as she unpacked a large box. "Could you please find them? There's so much they could be getting into around here."

"OK," Colby said, glad to have an excuse to leave the house for a while.

Where could those two be? Probably the stables—looking at the new colts. Colby started across to the brood mare barn.

The stable door was partly open for ventilation. Colby stepped inside and listened.

"I sure wish that colt was mine," Drew was saying, his voice carrying from the end of the barn.

"Someday I'm gonna have my own ranch and have all the horses I want," Dan said firmly.

"I'll help you run it," Drew said. "We can be partners. We can call it the Harris Ranch."

"Maybe we should ask Colby if he wants to run it with us," Drew suggested. "I'll bet he could get real good at breaking horses."

"Yeah, I know he'd like that," Dan said.

Colby smiled as he started toward them. He wondered if the twins had any idea how lucky they were. When they reached Colby's age, they'd hardly remember their old house in Sandsville. All they'd know would be ranch life —riding and roping. His dad had told them that the younger they learned to ride a horse, the better they could get at it.

But Colby didn't even dare talk about learning to ride a horse. After his ride on Pokey, he knew his dad would start his riding lessons *if* and *when* he chose.

6
BILLY

"Hey, you two. Mom's been wondering where you were and what you were getting into," Colby said, startling the twins as they watched a black mare nurse her new colt.

"Hi, Colby," Drew said glancing up. "Me and Dan are planning the ranch we're going to have when we get grown up. You want to be in on it with us?"

Colby grinned. "Let's see what Mom wants. Then you two can tell me your big plans."

"I'll beat you to the house," Drew shouted, taking off across the drive. Dan raced closely behind him.

Colby laughed as he watched his little brothers. His mom was right. The twins never got tired.

"It must be nice to have brothers."

Colby whirled around in the direction of the voice. He hadn't realized that anyone was around.

"Oh hi, Billy."

The dark-skinned boy was standing in the shadows of the barn.

"Sure. It's nice to have brothers. Sometimes they're little pests, but I guess I wouldn't want to trade them in or give them away."

Billy walked out into the sun.

"I sure wish I had a brother, or someone else in my family. Sometimes I think even a little sister wouldn't be so bad."

Colby wrinkled his nose. "I don't know about that. My mom says that she'd like to have a daughter, and I guess my dad would too. But Drew, Dan, and I are glad we have all boys in the family. You know, there's no girl stuff around."

Billy shrugged. "Yeah. Maybe you're right."

"I haven't seen you around much," Colby said.

"I got things to do," Billy said briefly. "Everybody in our family works. We're Mexican-Americans," he said loudly.

Colby was puzzled. He wasn't sure just what the boy meant, but one thing was certain. Billy had a pretty big chip on his shoulder for some reason.

"I hope my dad will let me do some ranch work," Colby said. "Getting to ride and rope sounds pretty neat."

"Yeah, well, don't get your hopes up too high," Billy warned. "Those are men's jobs, and you won't get to do much of the fun things around here anyway. Of course, since your dad's the foreman. . . ." Billy let his sentence die.

"What does your dad do?" Colby wanted to know.

"He's just a hand on the Two CC's." Billy looked embarrassed.

"I meant, what *kind* of ranch work," Colby explained.

"Oh, he's working one of the line shacks." Billy's eyes lit up with excitement.

"A line shack?" Colby asked.

"That's a cabin in the mountains where a hand spends three months taking care of one of the herds. Well, it's not really in the mountains, but there are lots of bluffs and hills," Billy explained. "Sometimes in the summer I get to go along if my dad gets summer duty. But he had to leave before school got out this time, so I had to stay with my mother and help her in the kitchen at the main house."

"You mean your father lives there in the mountains all by himself?" Colby wanted to know.

Billy nodded. "Yep. Sometimes Mr. Claypool or the foreman runs the lines and takes supplies and things to the men."

"Wow! That sounds great!"

"Yeah," Billy agreed, "you see and do things that you'd never get to do here at the ranch."

"Like what?"

"Well, once when I was trying to sleep, a chipmunk ran right over my blanket. Right across my belly. There aren't any windows in the cabin, just boards that you shut when it gets cold at night. And another time I was walking in the woods, and a deer and her fawn came right up to where I had stopped to rest. She'd probably never seen a person before, my dad told me. Baby deer are sure pretty little things."

Colby dug the toe of his boot into the dry ground. "It sure sounds like a great way to spend three months. Think there's any chance I'd get to go?"

Billy shrugged. "You might not like it. Cal didn't. Mr. Claypool made my father take him, and Cal hated it. Said he'd never go again." Billy spat on the ground in disgust. "Cal went instead of me. *I* should have gone."

"Well, I sure would like to go," Colby said. Then he added, "And, I don't think I'd hate it and want to come home, either."

"So, maybe you'll get to go. You're the foreman's son, aren't you?"

Colby looked at him sharply. That was the second time Billy had said that.

"Well, I got to be goin'. My mother wants me to pick some beans for dinner." Billy turned to go.

"Wait a minute," Colby said suddenly. He had to get something straightened out, once and for all. "I . . . I just want us to be friends," Colby began hesitantly. "Whatever my father does on this ranch has no connection with us being friends." He waited, but Billy just looked at him. "Let me be your friend like Cal is."

Billy jerked his head abruptly. "Cal is *not* my friend. He's nobody's friend. He thinks he's better than everyone—you, your brothers, and especially me."

Colby felt himself getting angry. "No one is any better than anyone else. We're all the same."

With a sarcastic laugh Billy thrust his brown arm out next to Colby's lightly tanned one. "That's the same?" he asked bitterly. "Maybe you don't see so good, huh?"

"I see," Colby replied evenly. "Just the same, I want to be your friend. We're all equal in God's sight. Your skin may be darker than mine, but that's the only difference between us."

"Ha!" Billy snorted. "You say so now. You live here awhile. Go to school in Rio Hondo. You'll change. You'll be just like everyone else." He turned and walked toward the main house.

Now what did I do? Colby wondered as he watched Billy a moment and then turned toward his own home. What would it be like to have darker skin than those around you? How would it feel to take for granted that other people were better than you?

Dear Lord, Colby prayed silently, *please help me to be a friend to Billy. Let me show him that You love him too.*

He started up the porch steps into the kitchen.

"You want to go fishing in the morning? There's a pond down by the main road."

Colby turned around. Billy was standing at the end of the long white porch. Colby shook his head and said, "I'd sure like to go, but tomorrow is Sunday. We always go to church on Sunday."

"Church?" Billy started to laugh. "Nobody goes to church around here." He turned and headed back in the direction he had come. His laughter filled Colby's ears— a laugh full of bitterness and pain.

Colby dropped into a kitchen chair. Ranch life wasn't at all what he'd expected. So many problems had popped up all at once, and he hadn't been a ranch kid even a week. Worse yet, he'd prayed that God would help him to be a friend to Billy. So just when he'd had a chance to start by going fishing, it had to be at a time when he couldn't go. Billy would think for sure that he had changed his mind.

And what was so funny about going to church in Rio Hondo, anyway?

7
CLASS OF THREE

"Boys, let me check your faces," Mrs. Harris ordered as the station wagon bumped down the lane from the ranch to the highway.

Colby automatically glanced at his own face in the rearview mirror as the twins held up their grinning faces for last minute inspection. He looked down at his Sunday pants and shirt. He sure hoped he looked right. He'd tried to get his mother to let him wear his new boots, but she had firmly vetoed that plan.

"Now, remember what I told you about our new church," his father reminded them all. "It will be a lot different from the one you're used to back home."

"We remember," Dan said leaning across the back of the front seat. "There probably won't be very many kids in our class, and maybe the room won't have a piano or be as nice as in our last church."

"But God will be there," Drew said, "and that's what is important."

46

"That's right," Mr. Harris agreed. "If just two or three people are in a place to worship God, He is there. The Bible promises us that."

"I hope there are more than two or three in my class, just the same," Colby said. "Can you imagine having a Bible drill or a party with just three kids?"

"Will you look at that!" Mrs. Harris exclaimed, pointing ahead on the road.

Mr. Harris put on the brakes and slowed the car. "I don't believe it," he said chuckling. "If it isn't Old Johnny Patton, his old horse, and buggy."

"Do you know who that man is?" Colby asked as he leaned forward for a better look at the old-fashioned buggy rolling down the road ahead of the car.

"I met the old fellow at the feed mill in town day before yesterday," Mr. Harris said. "Mr. Patton owns a little two-bit spread next to the Two CC's."

"How come he drives a horse and buggy?" Drew wanted to know.

"Yeah, doesn't he have a car?" Dan asked.

"What's *two-bit* mean?" Colby put in.

"Whoa boys," their father said, holding up his hand. "One question at a time. Johnny Patton drives a horse and buggy because he doesn't think the world needs the noise and confusion made by cars." He shrugged his shoulders. "Come to think of it, with all the air pollution and noise pollution, maybe he's right."

"He doesn't have a car at all? Honest, Dad?" Dan asked.

Mr. Harris shook his head. "Honest, he doesn't. As for your question, Colby, a two-bit spread is one that never amounts to much. I guess you don't hear it much anymore, but a bus ride used to cost two-bits in the city. That was two 12½ cent coins, or a quarter."

"I believe you lost me, Dear," Mrs. Harris said smiling. She turned to look out the car window as they drove slowly past the buggy and horse.

Mr. Harris raised his hand in greeting and the boys waved.

"Sure enough, it's Old Johnny," Mr. Harris said as they passed the elderly gentleman. "Since he's our neighbor, we may see him occasionally."

"I wonder where he's going," Colby said.

"Church, I expect," his father replied. "One thing I *do* know about Johnny Patton. He loves the Lord, and he tells everyone he meets about what God has done for him."

"It sure would be fun to ride in a buggy pulled by a horse," Colby said.

"There's the church up ahead," Dan shouted excitedly, pointing to the small white building up ahead.

In a few seconds, they arrived at the church. Colby surveyed the front of the church, while the rest of the family went ahead.

As he entered the big oak door, Colby tried hard to remember what his father had said about going to a small church. It looked like a church, the kind you saw on calendar pictures or magazine fronts with its white steeple and tall narrow windows. But there wasn't any carpeting on the floors. There was no organ, only a piano. The pews were real old-fashioned wooden ones without any padding. Was this really where they were going to go to church all the time? Colby couldn't believe it.

"Colby! Colby Harris!" Kevin Schwartz hurried around the back pew to greet him. "Boy, am I ever glad to see you! I thought maybe you wouldn't come."

"Dad said we would," Colby managed.

"I know," Kevin said, "but I thought . . . well, I thought that when you saw the church you might change your mind."

Colby nodded. "I know what you mean. It's sure not anything like our church back in Sandsville."

Kevin said, "My dad has all kinds of plans to change this place. And now that you're here, you can help. Dad says change has to come from within the church. He says that people have to get excited for God and then things get done."

Colby looked around the bare church. It looked cold and empty in spite of the hot weather and the few people gathered to worship. He sure couldn't imagine anyone getting very excited over living for God in this place.

He bit his bottom lip thoughtfully. His father had said that if just two or three people would agree to worship God any place, He would be there. And, if God was in a place, anything could happen.

Pastor Schwartz preached a good sermon, but it was hard for Colby to get his mind off his Sunday School class. Kevin's mother had taught the class. The lesson had been OK, but Colby had never been in a class of three people before. There had just been himself, Kevin, and a girl from town, Cindy Toleman, who had come with her grandmother. With the twins, there were only 11 kids in the whole Sunday School. There were a few more people who came in for the worship service. But still, there were only 27 people in church altogether. Colby counted them twice while they were singing a hymn.

After the service ended, Kevin hurried outside with Colby following.

"Man, am I ever glad you and your folks are coming to our church," Kevin began eagerly. "It's going to be a lot easier when I have help."

"Easier? What?" Colby asked uneasily.

"Building up our class, of course," Kevin said. "I've never gone to a church this small before either," he informed Colby. "But this is the only church in the area, and there is a lot of potential around Rio Hondo."

"A lot of what?" Colby wanted to know.

"A lot of people who could come to church. It's up to us to invite them," he said firmly.

"It is?"

"Sure," Kevin said. "It's up to us to let people know about God and get them interested in coming to church and learning about His Word. You are . . . I mean you have . . ." Kevin hesitated.

"You mean have I asked Jesus to forgive me for my sins?"

Kevin nodded.

"I have," Colby assured him.

"Then there's no problem," Kevin said. "My mom says that we can work up a list of kids we think might come to church. If we want, she'll let us have a party at our house. We'll play games, have pizza or something to eat, and then she'll tell a Bible story so the kids will kind of know what Sunday School is all about. Then we'll invite them to come to church the next Sunday."

"But I don't know anybody," Colby said lamely. "We just moved here, remember?"

"So did we," Kevin said grinning. "Our family moved to Rio Hondo two months ago, so I don't know many more kids than you do. But I do know there are some guys who live at your ranch. You could start with them. Will you ask them to come to church?"

Colby took a deep breath. "There *is* the boss' son, Cal, but he's . . . well, he isn't very friendly. Then there's Billy Sanchez. But I don't think he'd want to come to church from the way he talks."

"It couldn't hurt just to invite him, could it?" Kevin pushed.

Colby thought a moment. "I guess not."

"OK, then it's settled. I'll tell my mom what we're going to do, and I'll let you know when we can have a party," Kevin said. "Tell the guys about it too. Will you be at church tonight?" Silently, Colby nodded.

"See you later then," Kevin said hurrying to his father's car.

Colby was silent for the ride back to the ranch. It was bad enough that he had to come to a church that only had two other kids in his Sunday School class. But now he was supposed to help build up the class enrollment.

"This church is going to be a challenge for us," his mother was saying to his father. "There must be a real need for the Lord among the people of Rio Hondo."

His father chuckled. "The folks definitely aren't beating a path to the church doors. Still, I believe Pastor Schwartz has a real calling to this work. If we pray and witness to those we meet, I think God will draw people in Rio Hondo and the outlying ranches to Him."

Colby sighed. That was all right for his father to say. His dad hadn't agreed to invite Billy Sanchez to church. Right now Colby wasn't so sure he was going to be able to do it.

8
LEARNING TO RIDE

The delicious smell of ham, eggs, and freshly buttered toast drifted up the open stairs and right into Colby's bedroom. He stirred restlessly, and then sat up wide awake. Breakfast on the ranch was one thing he didn't want to miss.

Slabs of ham, sunny-side up fried eggs, golden brown potatoes, juice, fresh fruit . . . Colby's mouth watered at the thought of the feast waiting on the kitchen table. He grabbed his pants and shirt and dressed quickly. He raced for the bathroom, brushed his hair, and washed his face and hands, and then slid into his place at the table just seconds behind Dan and Drew.

"Are you boys extra hungry, or is there something exciting happening today that I don't know about yet?" Mrs. Harris asked.

"I'm starved," Colby said.

"Me too," Drew said as Dan nodded in agreement.

"Well, there's plenty for everyone," their mother assured them. She began putting the platters of food on the table.

"Talk about a group of lazy fellows," Mr. Harris said coming in the back door of the house. He grinned at his sons.

"Good morning, Dad," Colby said, looking up as his dad took a chair at the table. He knew his father had already put in several hours of work on the ranch.

Colby's mother took her chair. Then they all bowed their heads as Mr. Harris asked God's blessing on the food and His protection on their activities during the day.

"Pass the eggs, please," Drew asked the minute his father said "Amen."

Colby grinned and handed his little brother the platter without helping himself first. His father's prayer had reminded him of something. Not what he said, just the act of praying. Colby had wanted to mention the church party to Billy Sanchez the first thing Monday morning, but he hadn't gotten the chance. He had seen Billy several times, but somehow it hadn't seemed like the right time to bring up church.

Maybe he could invite Billy to Mrs. Schwartz' class party today, he told himself. Yes, he would do it today for sure. Colby took a bite of warm ham and chewed on the juicy tender meat. Everything seemed better about life on the Two CC's.

"Well, Son, ready to go?" his father said looking directly at him.

"Go? Where, Dad?" Colby asked eagerly.

"I guess it's about time we started those lessons we talked about some time ago," Mr. Harris said, a hint of a smile on his face.

Colby felt his throat tighten and a knot form in the pit of his stomach.

"Learn to ride?" he said, his voice almost a whisper.

His father nodded. "About time too. We might just need a fellow to run errands and carry messages, come branding time. You won't be firm in the saddle none too soon if we get started on it right now." He got to his feet, the chair scraping as he pushed it back from the table.

"Sure, Dad," Colby managed and tried to show some enthusiasm as he got up and went to put on his boots at the back door.

"Can we come?" the twins shouted, eager to watch.

Mr. Harris hesitated only a second. "Sure, come along. It won't be long before you two will be learning to ride too."

The twins chattered excitedly as they followed Colby and their father to the horse barn. Colby tried to get rid of that lump that was stuck in his throat. This was the moment he had been waiting for so long. Why wasn't he eager to learn to ride?

A chill ran down Colby's back in spite of the hot early morning sun. He couldn't forget his first ride—on Pokey. But riding with his father's supervision wouldn't be like that—at least that's what Colby tried to tell himself.

"You're so lucky," Dan said enviously as he watched Colby and Mr. Harris saddling the small black horse waiting in the stall.

"Is Hank really gentle?" Drew wanted to know, standing safely to one side as Colby and his father worked.

Mr. Harris nodded. "He's safe enough for you fellows to learn to ride on him."

Colby cleared his throat as he swung the cinch under Hank's belly for his father to secure on the opposite side. If Colby's father sensed his reluctance to ride, he certainly wasn't saying anything about it.

"All right, boys, stand back out of the way," Mr. Harris warned, taking the reins and backing the horse out of the stall and into the aisle. "I've saddled him for you this time, Colby, but from now on, it'll be up to you. I'll just check what you've done."

Colby nodded. He'd watched a lot of horses being saddled and readied for a day's work since he'd been at the Two CC's. He was pretty sure he could do it himself.

"Just remember that you want to make wearing a saddle as comfortable as possible for a horse so he'll enjoy himself. But you don't want the saddle to be so loose that it will slip around on his belly. A loose cinch has caused more than enough riding accidents."

"I'll remember, Dad," Colby promised.

"Why isn't the back strap tight?" Drew asked, pointing to the narrow leather strap under the back of Hank's stomach.

"It doesn't hold the saddle on the horse," Mr. Harris

explained. "It keeps it from flopping up and throwing a rider off when a horse runs or bucks. If the strap is too tight, it will be uncomfortable when the horse moves. But if it's too loose, it can cause a problem too. Sometimes a horse will have an itch on his stomach, just like we do."

"How does he scratch his itch?" Dan asked laughing.

"I know," Colby said. "The horse just reaches up with his hind leg and scratches."

"That's right," Mr. Harris said smiling. "And, if the back strap is too loose, a horse can catch his hoof in it and he'll probably break the strap and might break his leg in the process."

"You sure have to know a lot to ride a horse," Dan said.

That's the problem, Colby thought. *I don't know enough.*

"Well, let's get you up on this old fellow," his father said, turning to Colby.

"Uhhh, sure Dad," Colby said. He hitched up his jeans and pulled his hat down on his forehead. "I'm ready." His heart was beating so hard he was sure his dad could hear it above the sound of Hank's hoof beats on the hard dirt floor. The black horse obediently followed Mr. Harris to the door leading into the corral.

Colby's father stopped Hank and put the reins over the horse's neck. "Up you go, Son," he said.

Carefully, Colby put his boot in the stirrup and pulled himself up into the saddle. He hoped his dad couldn't see how his hands trembled as he picked up the reins. Colby didn't want to be scared, but he just couldn't help it. He

waited for his father to step out of the way and leave him to ride Hank alone—like Cal had done when Colby rode Pokey. But Mr. Harris stood right beside Hank.

"Now, just try to remember everything we've talked about, Son. It may be a little hard for you to get on a horse and ride right off, especially after what happened on your first ride."

Colby swallowed hard. How did his dad know how he felt?

"Just pick up the reins and nudge him gently with your heels. He'll walk right off," Mr. Harris said. "I'll be here."

Colby looked around the small riding area. Dan and Drew watched anxiously from the corral fence. Colby looked at his dad, meeting his brown eyes. He had to do it—to ride Hank—for his dad, for the twins, but most of all for himself.

Colby cautiously picked up the reins in his left hand and nudged Hank in the side just a bit. The horse started to walk around the ring just like his dad said. Automatically, Colby's right hand grabbed for the saddle horn to hold on.

"That's OK, Son," his father called out. "But Hank won't go anywhere. He knows you're just learning to ride, and he'll do what he's told."

Colby nodded. Suddenly, he realized that he had been holding his breath. He let it out slowly, and tried to relax. He let his body sway with the motion of Hank's walk. He watched the thick muscles rippling under the skin as the horse walked around the edge of the corral.

"You're doing just great!" Drew shouted.

"I'm going to learn to ride just like you," Dan said excitedly as Colby neared the fence where they sat watching.

"You're doing fine," Mr. Harris encouraged.

Colby took a deep breath and then he grinned.

Hank was every bit as gentle and wise an old horse as his dad had said. By the end of the first lesson, Colby was confidently mounting and dismounting. He could walk, trot, and back Hank when his father told him to.

"Always lead your horse into the barn," his father instructed as Colby took charge of unsaddling and brushing Hank down. "Never run a horse the last few hundred feet to the barn either. Choose a place, let's make it the ranch house, and slow down to a trot or walk there, before you come back to the barn. That way your horse will not be apt to charge through a half-open barn door and brush you off and hurt you."

"Dad, do you think I could ride Hank outside of the corral tomorrow?" Colby asked hesitantly. He thought he'd done pretty well at his first riding lesson, but he wasn't sure his father would think so.

"Do you think you're ready?"

"Well, I guess I am," Colby answered. "I'd like to try it anyway."

"Then I'll saddle up and we'll go for a ride on the range tomorrow," his father promised.

Colby could hardly contain his excitement as he carried

the saddle and bridle to the tack room. He hung up the
bridle and placed the blanket on top of the saddle to air
as his father had shown him.

"Hi."

Colby turned in surprise.

"I watched you," Billy said, standing in the doorway.
"You did all right. Your father is proud of you."

"You think so?" Colby wanted to know.

Billy nodded. "And, I'll tell you something. I think
there's a reason behind your dad teaching you to ride
right now."

"I know there is. He promised me I could learn to ride
when we first knew we were going to move to the Two
CC's Ranch."

Billy shook his head. "No, I mean why you're learning
to ride *now*, when your dad is so busy with all his other
duties."

"What do you mean?"

"Mr. Claypool was talking to my mother last night
after dinner. He's sending your dad up to the line shacks
with supplies the first of next week. Some of the men are
going along to check fences."

"You . . . you mean there might be a chance I'd get
to ride along?"

Billy nodded. He brushed his long black hair back over
his forehead. "Mr. Claypool told my mom there just
might be a chance I could go see my dad, if she didn't
mind. I bet your dad is teaching you to ride so he can
take you along too."

"Wow!" Colby closed and latched the tack room door. He felt like he would burst with excitement.

9
FRIENDS

"I guess I'll turn in," Colby said, yawning tiredly.

His mother looked up. "The twins were so tired they were asleep before I even left the room when I tucked them in."

"Well, see you in the morning." Colby got up and went to brush his teeth. And to think that he'd been worried about not having any real work to do on the ranch. He grinned to himself. He had blisters on his hands to show that he had cleaned his share of stalls and carried buckets of feed and water.

But the best part of each day was riding. He had taken to Hank like a duck to water, his dad had said. Colby sighed. His father even let him ride with Billy around the ranch. It felt great to lean forward in the saddle and nudge Hank into a canter. Colby shut his eyes and imagined the feel of the wind in his face as Hank ran in his smooth, rocking-chair motion.

He'd never dreamed he could be so happy living on a

ranch. Colby turned down the sheet and sat on the edge of the bed. As he reached for the Bible lying on the bedside table, he felt a twinge of guilt. He still hadn't asked either Cal or Billy to go to church, or even to go to the class party. He had promised Kevin—sort of, anyway.

Well, maybe he could ask Billy tomorrow. Cal was another problem. He almost never saw the ranch owner's son. Cal had friends from town, and he had made it pretty plain that he didn't care to make Colby a part of his group of friends.

Colby opened the Bible and read a chapter in the Old Testament. He had started to read the Bible all the way through when he had been in Mr. Eldon's Sunday School class back in Sandsville. Colby had read almost all of the Old Testament in the new Bible his parents had given him for his birthday. He liked to learn about the people who had lived in Bible times.

He rubbed his eyes as he finished reading and got down on his knees beside his bed to pray. He remembered to pray for Billy every night, but sometimes it was hard to remember to pray for Cal. It wasn't that he didn't like Cal Claypool, he just didn't know him very well. And the boss' son sure didn't go out of his way to make anyone like him.

Suddenly, Colby heard something hit the window screen. He got to his feet and hurried over to see what was causing the noise.

"Colby? Are you there?"

Colby looked down to the ground. The moon wasn't

very bright, but he could make out Billy's form two stories below, standing under his window.

"What do you want?"

"I want to talk to you," Billy whispered loudly.

"Can't it wait till tomorrow?"

Billy shook his head.

"Well, I'll go downstairs and meet you at the back door." Colby put on his clothes again and ran down the steps.

"I thought you went to bed," his mother said, looking up as he hurried through the living room.

"I did," Colby replied. "But Billy wants to talk to me."

"It's getting late," his father warned.

"It won't take long, Dad."

As soon as Colby opened the back door, Billy stepped inside. He looked around nervously.

"Are your folks up?"

Colby nodded. "They're in the living room. What's so important that it couldn't wait till morning?"

Billy stared at the floor nervously. "It's Cal. . . ."

Colby sighed. "You're going to have to tell me. That IS what you came for, isn't it? How can I help if you won't say what happened?"

Billy scratched his hand and rubbed his shoulder, shifting from one foot to the other.

"You . . . you know how Cal is," he began.

"Not really," Colby said. "I hardly know him, and he hasn't made any effort to change that since I've been here."

"Well, he's always getting me to do things that he ought to do," Billy said finally. "Lots of times I've cleaned the barns when Cal should have, just because he told me to. Sometimes when things get lost or misplaced, Cal blames me for it, and I get into trouble with Mr. Claypool." Billy bit his bottom lip nervously. "Well, tonight Mr. Claypool told Cal to haul those feed sacks of grain from the wagon to the grain bin before Cal went to town with Randy and Bob."

Colby nodded. He had seen Cal getting into Bob Morgan's pickup and leaving for town after dinner. "Did Cal tell you to empty the grain wagon?"

Billy nodded. "I told him I didn't have time. My mom wanted me to do some chores after dinner. Cal said if I didn't do it, he'd make me wish I had." Billy hesitated. "He called me a lot of nasty names. I decided that I wasn't going to unload that wagon for him. It's a lot of work."

Colby thought about what Billy had said. He knew that the grain bags were heavy—he had tried to carry the specially mixed horse feed once. "So what did you do?" Colby asked.

"Nothin'," Billy said. "I just did the chores like my mom said. I forgot all about Cal telling me to do his work."

"I still don't see what the problem is," Colby said impatiently.

"Me and Mom were sitting at the table talking about sending Pa some supplies when I heard Cal yelling and storming out of the big house."

"Honest?" Colby's eyes grew big.

Billy nodded. "And the next thing, he was at the door. He told me to come outside. I didn't know what else to do, so I stepped off the porch. And then Cal told me that he was going to make me mighty sorry that I hadn't done what he said."

Billy swallowed hard, his eyes filled with fright. "I don't like Cal's friends. They're so much older than Cal is, and just plain mean. I don't want any of them beating up on me."

"Is that what Cal said they'd do?" Colby asked, feeling afraid himself.

Billy nodded.

Colby took a deep breath. "Can't you tell your mom? Couldn't she tell Mr. Claypool that Cal had threatened you?"

Billy shook his head. "I didn't tell her, and I'm not going to either. It wouldn't do any good. Besides, she'd just worry."

"Well, my dad's not afraid of Cal," Colby said firmly. "You don't have to worry about that. He'll take care of things."

"Oh no, you can't do that!"

"Why not?" Colby looked puzzled.

"You just can't. Promise me that you won't say a word to anyone. Promise me!"

"All right," Colby promised reluctantly, "if you really want me to. But it would solve everything if you'd let me tell my dad that Cal had threatened you."

"No!" Billy said heatedly. "You don't understand. It's not the same for you as it is for me. What happens to me doesn't matter."

"Well, it matters to me," Colby said.

Billy looked up in surprise.

"I'm going to do my best to see that nothing happens to you," Colby promised.

Billy stared solemnly at Colby for a long time.

"I've got to go," he said suddenly. He opened the door and slipped out into the darkness.

Colby slowly closed the door and walked through the kitchen. There was no one in the living room. He could hear water running in the bathtub. Quickly, he hurried up to his room. He was glad neither of his parents had been around to question him about Billy's late night visit.

He knelt beside his bed to add a quick P.S. to his prayer.

"Dear Lord, help Billy and me tomorrow. No matter what Cal has in mind, please make things work out all right. And help me to invite Billy to church too."

Colby got up and turned out the light on the bedside table. Billy was right. Colby didn't understand. He knew what his new friend meant, though. He remembered well the first time he had seen Cal Claypool. The boss' son had tossed the dark-skinned boy the reins of his horse and ordered him to take care of the animal, just as if Billy were his servant.

Billy Sanchez is no less a person because his skin is a little darker than someone else's, Colby thought angrily. *And, it is time Cal Claypool learned that.*

10 THE FIGHT

For some reason the eggs and ham didn't taste so good. Colby pushed back his chair and excused himself from the table.

"Anything special for me to do today, Dad?" he asked.

Mr. Harris nodded. "That big bay mare is due to foal. I want you to clean the box stall on the far end and get it ready for her and the new baby."

"Another new baby?" Dan asked excitedly.

Mrs. Harris smiled. "Sometimes I wonder if you boys will ever get used to having animals arrive around the clock. Seems like the excitement should wear off someday."

"I'll tell you a secret," Mr. Harris said, grinning at the twins. "Your mother is one of the first ones out in the barns when there's a new colt on the ground. Don't let her fool you."

"Oh, James," she said.

Colby pulled his boots on and walked across the drive

to the horse barn. He opened the grain door and began filling the feed pail. It was his job to feed the brood mares in the barn each morning, and to be sure their waterers were working, and that there was plenty of hay available.

He hadn't slept too well the night before. It was all because of Billy. What had ever made Colby say he'd stand up for Billy against Cal Claypool? Of course Cal didn't have any right to push Billy around just because he was a Mexican-American. But how stupid could a guy get? Colby didn't have a chance against Cal, or even one of those bullies he called friends.

A chorus of nickers and soft-throated noises from the mares greeted Colby as he walked down the barn aisle between the box stalls. After the horses had eaten, Cal or one of the hands would turn them into the corrals for exercise.

He hadn't seen a sign of Cal anywhere—or his horse. Colby finished his feeding chores and got the wheelbarrow and pitchfork to start working on the box stall for the bay mare. All the stalls were cleaned regularly, so it wasn't much work to take out the small amount of soiled straw and wood chips on the floor.

"Hi, want some help?" Billy asked as he leaned over the stall door.

"Sure," Colby answered.

Billy raked the floor while Colby went for a bale of fresh straw. The stall had to be clean and absolutely safe for the new baby colt that would be born.

"Wanna go for a long ride today?" Billy asked as Colby shook some straw around the box.

"You mean by ourselves—on the range?"

Billy nodded. "I know a real great place to go. There's a deserted mine over on the old Patton place. All the kids ride over there and go exploring."

"Wow! That sounds great!" Colby stopped abruptly. "I don't know if Dad will let me go that far alone."

"Oh, Hank is a plug. Nothing in the world could happen to you on that old horse."

"Watch how you talk about my mount," Colby said sternly, but he grinned. "I guess you're right. I think my little brothers could ride him safely. He may be reliable, but he's not a plug. Hank is a super cow horse. My dad said so."

"OK, OK. I take it all back," Billy said, grabbing straw to help. "But there isn't any reason why we couldn't ride alone today. At least you could ask."

"You're right," Colby agreed.

"That's good enough," Billy said, swinging his foot to level out the ankle-deep layer of straw. "Just like a feather bed."

"Aw, what do you know about feather beds?" Colby asked teasingly.

"Well, I've read about them," Billy said, grinning. "Now come on, let's go find your dad. I'd just as soon get away from this place before anything happens."

Colby wrinkled his nose thoughtfully. "That just might be a good idea. No sense waiting around for trouble."

Mr. Harris was in the house sitting at the kitchen table, writing a report when Billy and Colby found him.

"Dad, Billy wants me to go on a ride with him. We'd need a lunch and we'd be gone most of the day. Could I go, please, Dad?" Colby asked.

Mr. Harris looked up.

"Oh, Colby, his mother said. She was kneading bread dough in a large bowl. "You don't ride well enough yet to go off by yourself."

"Hank is as safe a horse as there is, Mom. Dad told me so. And we'll be careful."

"Yes," Mr. Harris said slowly. "I think it would be all right. Hank is as reliable an animal as you'll find anywhere. Besides, Colby has got to go on his own sometime." He smiled at his wife.

"Wow! Thanks, Dad," Colby shouted. He turned and raced out of the house toward the barn with Billy following.

"Stop back by the house when you're ready to go, and I'll have a lunch waiting," his mother called after them.

The sun beat down warmly on their heads and shoulders as the two boys rode across the range. Colby rested his hand lightly on Hank's thick black mane. If only his friends could see him now, riding the range on a beautiful horse. He smiled contentedly to himself.

"What's so funny?" Billy wanted to know.

Colby shrugged. "Nothin' I guess. I was just thinking about my friends back in Sandsville. Ranching sure isn't what I expected it to be. It's a lot better."

"Sure, the work and all," Billy said dryly.

"Oh, it's not so bad, and when we go to school, we won't have nearly so much to do," Colby said. "By the way, speaking of work, how about taking time off to go to a party?"

"What kind of a party?"

"Well I guess an 'eating' party—you know, the kind where you play games and maybe have a hot dog roast or a barbecue and softball game."

"I don't think so," Billy said slowly.

"It would be fun," Colby said. "We always had fun at our Sunday School class parties back where I used to go to church."

"Oh, you didn't say it was a church party," Billy said accusingly.

"I bet you would like it anyway," Colby encouraged. "There won't be a whole lot of people there, and Kevin Schwartz, our pastor's son, is a nice guy."

Billy didn't answer for a moment.

"Naw, I guess not," he finally said, breaking the silence.

They rode on, listening to the muffled sound of the horses' hooves on the dry ground. *Well, I blew it*, Colby thought miserably. *Maybe it wasn't the right time to ask Billy to the church party. Maybe I should have prayed more about it.*

"Oh no!" Billy said suddenly. "Look who's coming!"

Colby followed Billy's gaze and his heart dropped clear to the bottom of his stomach. Two riders were cantering across the range toward them, and the horse in the lead was definitely the big buckskin, Ham Bone.

"What'll we do?" Billy asked. He had a terrified look on his face.

Colby reined in Hank. "Just keep calm," he instructed. His own heart was beating so hard he was sure his shirt was jumping up and down.

"Well, fancy meeting you two here," Cal said, a smirk growing on his lips.

"Yeah, a nice coincidence, seeing you and Billy had planned to have that little talk today," Bob, the second rider, said.

Colby nudged Hank in front of Billy's bay mare.

"Why don't you go pick on somebody your own size, Cal," Colby said, trying to joke.

"And why don't you just stay out of the way?" Cal growled, his eyes narrowing as he stared straight at Colby. "I don't have any quarrel with the foreman's son, but I do with this little jerk." He pointed a finger at Billy. "He don't know how to do what he's told."

"It's not Billy's job to do your chores," Colby said, feeling braver as his face grew red with anger. "Emptying that grain wagon was hard work, too hard for you to want to do or you wouldn't have tried to force Billy to do it."

"Who's speaking to you?" Cal shouted. "Now get out of our way. We've got a score to settle with a punk that don't know his place on this ranch."

Cal kicked Ham Bone in the sides and rode in front of

Colby over to Billy. Then Cal reached down to grab the reins of Billy's horse.

"Leave him alone," Colby shouted, grabbing at Cal's hand. "Get out of here, Billy!" he ordered. But it was too late; Cal had grabbed the bridle reins to Conchita, Billy's horse.

Out of the corner of his eyes, Colby saw Bob raise a riding whip and bring it down as hard as he could across Hank's hind quarters. The horse half reared in surprise and tore crazily across the range. Colby gripped the saddle horn with both hands. He was too terrified to reach for the reins hanging across Hank's neck to try to control the runaway horse.

Suddenly, Hank veered to avoid a scrub bush and Colby

felt his hands lose their grip on the saddle horn. He flew through the air, and then hit the ground.

Colby tried to move, but he couldn't breathe. It felt like someone was sitting on his chest. Somewhere in the distance, he could hear shouts. He had to get up to go help Billy, but he couldn't move.

Finally, he pulled himself up to a halfway sitting position, leaning on an elbow. He tried to look around. He saw Hank nearby. The horse was contentedly munching a clump of dry grass, as if nothing had happened.

Just then Colby heard a loud sound like a war-whoop. Slowly, he turned his head just in time to see Cal and his friend galloping off across the range. But where was Billy? There was Conchita, standing off to one side. Then Colby saw his friend, lying on the ground, motionless.

11
THE
PROMISE

"Billy!" Colby called loudly. He took a deep breath and winced at the sharp pain in his chest. *What had Cal done to Billy?*

"Billy? Can you hear me?"

For a moment, Colby thought he saw Billy move, then he wasn't sure. Painfully, he got to his feet. His right ankle hurt. He must have twisted it when he fell, but he could walk on it. He walked slowly toward Hank. He reached out for the reins. Hank turned his head and moved just out of reach.

Colby sighed and followed the black horse. He tried to grab the reins quicker this time, but Hank wouldn't allow himself to be caught. Colby started to walk over to where Billy lay. His ankle throbbed with each step. *Why didn't Billy get up? Was he unconscious?*

"Billy? Billy, are you all right?" he called as he hobbled up to where his friend lay on the ground. He dropped to his knees beside him.

78

"Can you hear me?" he shouted.

Billy moaned and stirred slightly.

At least he's alive, Colby thought with relief. He sure looked a mess. One eye was puffed up. A trickle of blood still flowed over the caked-on mess where Billy had been hit in the nose. His bottom lip was cracked and swollen.

Colby kept talking to him, and at last Billy started to come around.

"They're gone, Billy," he reassured him as his friend opened his eyes at last. "Do you think you're all right?"

"Ohhh," Billy moaned. "My head hurts."

"There's a big bump on your forehead, like someone hit you with something hard." Colby helped as Billy tried to sit up.

He held his head in his hands, moaning softly.

"Can you ride?" Colby asked after a moment.

Billy looked up. "Sure, if I can walk," he said, trying to smile through his swollen lips.

"I can't catch Hank," Colby said. "Do you think your horse will ride double?"

Billy nodded. "I feel so weak. I guess that's what happens when you get beaten up."

"Don't feel bad," Colby said. "I don't see that you had any choice in the matter. I'd have stayed to help but Bob hit Hank with his whip. I didn't get him stopped before Hank dumped me. But that wasn't really the horse's fault. I'm getting pretty good at falling off, though." Colby smiled. "I seem to get plenty of practice at it."

"Colby?" Billy spoke his name with a different tone. "You're OK as far as I'm concerned," Billy said; then he struggled to his feet and walked over to Conchita. It was several painful minutes before Billy hauled himself up into the saddle.

"I . . . I don't know if I can get up behind you the way this ankle of mine feels," Colby said. Then he laughed. "We make quite a pair."

Just then, Colby felt a nudge in his side. It was Hank. Quickly, he grabbed the reins hanging from the black horse's bridle.

"I don't get it," Colby said, puzzled. "He wouldn't let me touch him a minute ago."

Billy tried to smile through his sore lips. "He is jealous, that's all. A lot of horses are like that. They can't stand it when another horse gets attention, even if they'd rather be free to graze than be ridden. They will come to you if you even look at another horse."

"Well, I'll be," Colby said in amazement. "With Hank it'll at least be easier to get back to the ranch."

Billy turned his horse in the direction of the ranch. He braced himself against the saddle horn to ease the pain of jolting in the saddle.

"I sure feel weak."

"Hey, wait a minute. We haven't eaten lunch, and Mom sent a lot of stuff. I know we'll feel better if we get some food in our stomachs." Colby reached for the saddlebags behind the saddle.

All they lacked was something to drink, but they felt a

lot better once they had eaten. The horses stood patiently until the last sandwich was gone and all the cookies had been eaten.

"I guess we'd better go," Colby said finally.

Billy nodded.

It was a long trip back to the ranch. Neither boy felt like going any faster than a walk. Even that hurt their sore muscles. There wasn't much conversation either. Billy's face was looking worse all the time, and he had a hard time talking through his swollen lips.

"What do you think Mr. Claypool will say when he finds out what Cal did to you?" Colby asked as they started down the lane to the horse barn.

Billy shook his head. "I won't tell him."

"Are you serious?" Colby asked in amazement. "You're just going to let that big bully pound on you and not say a word?"

Billy nodded. "I won't tell on him."

"Well, you can keep quiet all you want to," Colby said angrily, "but *I'm* going to make sure that Mr. Claypool hears about this!"

"No!"

Colby turned his head sharply to look at him. "Are you crazy?"

Billy shook his head. "Promise you won't tell."

Colby bit his lip. "All right, I promise," he said finally, against his better judgment.

A look of relief came over Billy's face.

"But I want you to know I'm keeping my mouth shut

against my will, against what I think I should do." Colby frowned. "I just can't believe that Mr. Claypool would let Cal do anything more to you if he knew the truth."

"You don't know," Billy said ominously.

Colby sighed deeply. There didn't seem to be any answer.

At the barn door both boys eased themselves gently out of their saddles. Colby noticed that Billy had a hard time walking upright. Cal must have hit him pretty hard in the stomach.

"I'll put your gear away," he offered as soon as Billy had unsaddled his mare.

"Thanks," Billy said. He turned and started toward the door.

Colby took a deep breath and picked up Hank's saddle. All he wanted was to lie down and rest for a while. Then he'd feel better. His ankle still hurt awfully bad, but the more he used it, the better it felt. He'd be all right, but what about Billy?

It seemed to take forever before he had put everything away and the horses were in their stalls. Colby closed the tack room door and started toward the barn. It would be pretty hard not to say anything about what had happened. Colby wasn't used to keeping secrets from his parents. But Billy trusted him.

12
TWINS!

"Colby. Colby!"

Colby turned over in his sleep. He could feel someone gently shaking him. His body was still asleep. It hurt to move. Groggily, he opened his eyes and saw his father's face in the light of the bedside lamp. He looked out the window.

"It isn't time to get up yet," he mumbled, trying to cover his head with the sheet. "It's dark out."

"There's something I want you to see," his father said, continuing to shake him awake.

"Now?"

"Come on, Son, get dressed," his father urged. "You may never get to see anything like this again in your entire lifetime. It's a first for me too."

In a flash Colby was pulling on his pants and throwing a shirt over his shoulders. He slipped his bare feet into his boots at the back door and followed his father out into the warm night.

It was beautiful outside. Colby glanced up at the bright stars as he hurried to the barn, buttoning his shirt on the go. The surprise had to be pretty special for his dad to haul him out of bed in the middle of the night. He followed his father through the door into the dimly lit barn.

His mother was there, at the back stall, in her robe. She turned and smiled without saying a word. Colby quickened his steps and leaned over the stall door to see what the surprise was.

"Ohhh," he mouthed wordlessly. He stared, wide-eyed into the stall.

There on the straw lay two small look-alike colts. As Colby watched, the mother nuzzled her newborn babies with her moist black nose.

"They've already been up and nursed," Mrs. Harris said, her quiet voice betraying her excitement.

"How old are they, Dad?" Colby asked.

"About two hours," Mr. Harris said, grinning. "Doc Peters has been here and gone already, but your mother and I thought that this special event was one that you shouldn't miss. There'll be time enough for Dan and Drew's racket in the morning."

Colby nodded. "They'd be so crazy with excitement they'd drive any new mother nuts," he agreed.

"For a horse to have twins is very rare," Mrs. Harris said as she stood looking at the mare and her two darling babies. "I can only remember seeing one set of twin horses in my life. They were painted colts, spotted almost identically."

"It is special for them to be born, and even more miraculous for them to live," his father explained. "Only about one percent of all twins born survive."

"Wow, then these are pretty special," Colby said.

"You're right about that, Son."

Colby turned as Mr. Claypool came up to the stall. Colby moved back so the Two CC's boss could get another look at his new colts.

"Doc Peters says this is only the second pair of twins he's helped bring into the world in his entire career, and the only pair where they both lived long enough to get on their feet and eat," Mr. Claypool informed them.

"Well, these two seem healthy enough," Mr. Harris said. "For the fact that there are two of them, they're good sized and well formed. I'd say you've got a bargain this time."

"I wish Billy could see the twins," Colby said without thinking.

"Well, I suppose you could go wake him up," his mother said slowly. "His mother probably wouldn't mind since this is so special."

"Aww, I don't know," Colby stalled. Why had he thought aloud? He knew Billy would love to see the twin colts, but he didn't want anyone to see Billy the way he looked. How could he be so dumb? The last person Billy would want to see would be Mr. Claypool.

"I guess I won't bother him," Colby said at last. "He's seen a lot of horses. Tomorrow morning will be soon enough."

"Speaking of morning, you'd better go back to bed. You don't want to be tired for church tomorrow," his mother said, giving him a pat on his shoulder.

"You mean today," Colby said, grinning.

His mother nodded. "Whatever, back to bed with you." She looked in the stall once more, and Colby crowded between his folks to get another look.

It seemed as if Colby had hardly shut his eyes when his mother was waking him to get up for church. Breakfast and the rest of the Sunday morning routine went by more quickly than usual. Even the ride to church seemed to take less time than last week.

Before he knew what had happened, Colby found himself in his Sunday School room. He looked around the small classroom. Kevin wasn't there yet. In a way, Colby wished he didn't have to face him. *Maybe Kevin didn't have any luck in asking anyone to come to church either,* Colby half hoped to himself.

Just then the door opened and Kevin walked into the room.

"Hi, Colby. I want you to meet David and Mark Lansing," Kevin said, grinning from ear to ear.

Colby tried to smile in return, but it was more of a gulp than anything else.

"Did you get to talk to Cal Claypool or Billy Sanchez?" Kevin whispered as his mother came into the room to begin the Sunday School lesson.

"No," he said, his face getting red from the neck up. "I . . . I just didn't find the right time to do it."

"Oh." Kevin's disappointment was apparent. "Well, maybe you'll be able to ask them this week."

Colby nodded.

There were a number of new people in church. Colby looked around during the worship service. He really felt rotten because he hadn't done his part. Everyone else had seemed to. He knew his parents witnessed to people regularly and invited them to church. Why did he find it so hard? Maybe it would be easier when he started school in the fall. It was hard to ask people you hardly knew to church, and even harder to tell them about God.

But Kevin had done it.

After church Mrs. Harris suggested that Colby ask Kevin home with them for dinner. Kevin's folks agreed that it was OK, and soon they were riding in the car toward the Two CC's Ranch.

"I've always wanted to live on a real ranch," Kevin said.

"We all have too," Colby said. "Dad used to live on the Baker Ranch near here, before he married my mom. He always planned to bring us back here, and he finally did."

"Hey, you can see the new twin colts," Drew said, turning with excitement to Kevin.

"That's right," Colby said, remembering. "One of the mares had twins last night. Dad says it's a real miracle. They both lived and are healthy."

"They're pretty neat," Dan added. "You want to see them?"

Kevin nodded. "I'd like to see everything on the Two CC's Ranch."

After dinner the boys all hurried out to the foaling barn to see the new colts.

"Wow!" Kevin said quietly, staring over the stall door at the babies. "They're something else."

"I got to see them when they were only a couple of hours old," Colby told him. "Dad woke me up in the middle of the night to come to the barn."

"I'd sure like to live around horses," Kevin said wistfully.

"Horses aren't the only animals that are bred and raised here," Colby said importantly. "The ranch has some of the best cattle around. Some as good as the cattle raised on the Mason Ranch."

"Honest?" Kevin asked, obviously impressed.

Colby nodded.

"Do you get to ride horses?" Kevin asked.

"Of course," Colby answered. "Well," he grinned sheepishly, "I'm learning. I know it will be awhile before I'm very good at it."

"Do you think I could ride a horse?" Kevin wanted to know.

"Sure. I'll get Hank out and saddle him up for you."

Suddenly, Colby stopped short. Hank wasn't his horse. He had no business letting Kevin ride him. He was always going ahead without asking permission. That's how he often got himself into trouble.

"I . . . I think we'd better ask my dad first," Colby said. "He's pretty strict about who rides what around here."

Kevin hesitated, obviously disappointed, then he nodded.

"I guess you're right. Do you think he'll let me ride?" Kevin asked.

"Let's go ask," Colby suggested.

He turned around to go to the house, then he stopped. His father was standing in the barn door.

"I think we need to have a talk, Colby," his father said, sternly.

"Sure." Colby's heart was beating rapidly. "What about, Dad?" He knew his voice was shaking.

"About Billy Sanchez."

13
A BROKEN PROMISE

It seemed as if his father asked him a hundred questions as Colby sat in the living room, staring out the window. *How could a guy obey his father and still remain loyal to a friend?* His father had wanted to know about the fight on the range.

Mrs. Sanchez had come to Mr. Harris instead of Mr. Claypool because she was afraid of what Cal might do to Billy in the future, his father had explained to Colby.

"It's not as if you'll be snitching on your friend, Son," Mr. Harris had said gently. "I already know there was a fight. I just need to get to the bottom of it so I can help Billy."

What if he didn't tell and Billy got hurt because Cal was allowed to go unpunished for his deeds? It was a hard decision.

"OK, Dad," he finally said slowly. "I guess I first noticed how Cal treated Billy when we pulled into the Two CC's the first day. And, the worst part of it is that Cal has Billy convinced that he's not as good as everyone else."

Mr. Harris frowned. "I don't think I understand what you mean, Colby."

"Well, it's because Billy's skin is darker than ours, and maybe because his hair is so black and straight." Colby shrugged. "Oh, I don't know," he said miserably. "I guess it's because Billy is a Mexican-American."

"I've never seen José Sanchez," Mr. Harris said thoughtfully, "but from what Mr. Claypool has said, Billy's father is a fine hand, a responsible line shackman, and a capable horse trainer."

"Well, I sure wish someone would tell Cal Claypool," Colby said sighing. "He makes life rough for Billy, conning him into doing all his chores." He hesitated. "Well, maybe not all of them, but the worst ones."

"I'm glad you've confided in me," his father said. "I realize it was a hard thing to do. I want you to tell Billy that you have talked with me. I don't know what I'm going to do as yet, but *something* will have to be done. We can't have anyone—the boss' son or anyone else— causing trouble like this on a working ranch."

"You . . . you won't go to Cal's father, will you, Dad?"

Mr. Harris ran his hand through his hair thoughtfully. "I don't think so, not yet anyway. This is something that needs prayer—so I will have the wisdom to deal with it in the right way."

Colby sighed. That was a relief. But what good would it do to pray? Cal didn't even act like he believed in God.

And Colby wasn't all that sure about Billy either.

Colby got up from the chair and turned to go. "Is that all, Dad?"

Mr. Harris closed his eyes briefly. Then he looked at Colby with a smile on his face. "I think I have the perfect solution for the moment, anyway."

"What do you mean?"

"Well," Mr. Harris drawled, "I plan to make the rounds of the line shacks this week. In fact, I think I'll start first thing tomorrow morning."

"But what's that got to do with Cal and Billy?"

Mr. Harris paused, a twinkle appearing in his brown eyes.

"It's been a long time since Billy has spent any time with his father. Sometimes when a fellow has a problem, it helps to talk it over with his dad. Know what I mean?"

Colby nodded. "Sure, but what's that got to do..." Suddenly he smiled. "You're going to take Billy along on the trail ride!" he said.

"That's exactly what I'm going to do, that is, if Mrs. Sanchez will allow it."

"Oh, I'm sure she would," Colby assured his father. "Billy told me that he's gone with his dad to the line shack before. The only reason he couldn't go this time was that his father had to leave before school was out for the summer."

"So you think that might be the answer to the problem right now?" Mr. Harris asked.

Colby nodded.

"I do too," his father agreed. "It will get Billy away from Cal long enough to cool things down. He'll have a chance to talk with his father, and I'll be able to discuss it with them both. Then I may have a better idea how to talk with Cal and his father about it." He sighed. "Yes, I think a young fellow would enjoy the trip to the line shack."

Colby sighed, trying to hide his disappointment. He'd hoped that his father would let him go along. But he wasn't a good enough rider to take a trip into the mountains. He'd just have to wait. Maybe next year.

"Is something wrong, Son?" Mr. Harris asked.

"No, Dad," Colby shook his head. "I was just thinking that any guy would like to make the trip up to the line shacks. You know what? Billy told me about seeing a mother deer and her fawn drinking at a mountain stream. He said a chipmunk even ran right across his blanket during the night once."

"Uh huh," his father said, nodding his head. "I think you'll have a good time and learn more about ranching than I could cram into your head on the ranch here in an entire summer."

"Honest, Dad? You mean I get to go too?" Colby shouted excitedly.

"Oh?" His father had a surprised look on his face, but his eyes were twinkling. "Didn't I tell you that I planned to take both you and Billy along?"

"Wow! Thanks, Dad! Thanks a lot!" He started toward the door. "I've got to go tell Billy and Kevin."

He saw Kevin and the twins at the corral watching the mares and foals as he raced across the drive to the big house.

"I'll be there in a minute," he shouted.

Kevin waved in return.

"Billy! Billy!" He pounded on the screen door.

It seemed forever before Billy came to the door. Through the black screening his face looked horrible, all bruised and swollen.

"How . . . how are you feeling?" Colby asked first.

Billy opened the door to let him in. "OK, I guess," he mumbled.

"Hello, Mrs. Sanchez," Colby said, smiling at Billy's mother. "I've got great news," he said turning back to Billy. "But first I guess I'd better explain."

As Colby told about his talk with his father, Billy's dark eyes grew black with anger.

"You promised!" he hissed.

"It wasn't all Colby's fault," Mrs. Sanchez said, coming over to Billy. "I talked with Mr. Harris."

Billy glared at his mother.

"No, Son, you shouldn't look at me like that," she reprimanded. "It is my right to do what I feel is best for you. You are the man of this house when your father is away. I need you. I cannot allow you to be hurt or injured because of a spoiled boy who must have his way all the time."

Slowly, the anger in Billy's eyes faded.

"I had to tell you that, in order to tell you what my

father has decided," Colby explained. "Tomorrow morning he is going to leave for the supply trip to the line shacks."

Billy's eyes lit up with sudden interest.

"Dad thought it might be good if you and Cal weren't around each other until things cool off. So he's going to take you and me with him on the trip to the mountains." Colby swallowed hard. "Well, if your mother will let you go."

"Mother?" Billy turned to look at Mrs. Sanchez.

"Of course, Son," she said smiling broadly. "In fact, if I were not needed here to cook and clean, I would like to go along with you." She sighed. "I used to go to the line shacks with my man, you know."

"Well, I have to go. Kevin came home with me from church to have dinner. He's at the colt exercise corral with Dan and Drew. I'd better be company for him," Colby said. "Want to come along, Billy?"

Billy hesitated. "No. Thanks anyway."

"I think not also, Colby," Mrs. Sanchez said. "There is much work to be done if Billy is to be ready to go see his father. There are many things that I want to send to my man, and tasks that must be done before my second man leaves me alone."

"I'll see you in the morning then," Colby said, turning to leave.

He hurried off the long narrow porch and started across the drive to find Kevin and the twins. Tomorrow he would be on Hank, riding across the range on the long trail ride into the mountain pasture range.

Colby could hardly believe it. His dad had actually decided that he could ride well enough to go along. Billy had suggested that he would be ready, but he hadn't known he was.

He threw his arms in the air and shouted, "Yippee!"

14
MOVIN' OUT

Colby was so excited that he had a hard time swallowing breakfast. He had been up before the sun, helping his dad gather supplies and rig up the pack horses for the trip. His father would ride Big Red, the horse he had chosen to be his working mount until he could find and train a horse just for himself.

Billy would ride Conchita, and Colby would ride Hank. Al and Darrell, two ranch hands, would lead the pack train of six horses that carried the supplies to the men stationed in the line shacks.

Colby stuffed the last bite of waffle into his mouth and excused himself. He pulled on his boots and hurried outside. Al and Mr. Harris were packing the boxes of food and goods. There were blankets, fresh clothes, boots, and personal things for the men. There was one stack of magazines, and a whole box of books.

"Run in and ask your mother to find a roll of tape," Mr. Harris called to Colby.

spread fresh bedding on the last stall. "You look better this morning."

Billy paused and gingerly touched his swollen eye with his fingertips.

"At least I slept last night without waking up," Billy said. It was still hard for him to talk.

"Dad says we'd better get the horses saddled," Colby said.

"Well, I'm done here." Billy set the rake and pitchfork in the aisle outside the stall.

"Wanna look at the colts once more before we go?" Colby asked.

Billy grinned. "Sure."

The big bay mare eyed the boys curiously as they leaned over the stall. She was quite used to the attention. In fact, she appeared to like visitors. The colts were resting on the straw bedding.

"They sure are something, aren't they?" Billy said softly.

Colby looked sharply at his friend. He'd never heard Billy sound like that before. "They are," he agreed.

Billy shook his head. "We'd better get over to the other barn. Your dad won't be too happy if we hold things up."

The boys and Mr. Harris checked and rechecked their gear. It would be a long ride. It would take at least two-and-one-half days to reach the first line shack. They'd be gone two full weeks—if everything went all right.

Colby wrapped his jacket and spare clothes in his bedroll. His dad showed him how to fasten it in back of his saddle. Colby knew he would learn a lot on this ride. Already he knew so much more about what to take on a trail ride and what kind of supplies a man needed in a line shack.

They would be checking fences and water holes as they rode along. The hands with the pack horses would go right to the line shacks to deliver the supplies. Colby shivered with excitement at the thought of sleeping under the stars and cooking over an open campfire. His father's horse carried all their extra gear. They would meet up with the pack-horse train when they could.

Mr. Harris went to Billy and gave Conchita a final thorough check. "Looks like you're all ready to go, Billy."

"Thank you, Sir," Billy said.

"Looks like you've done all right too," Mr. Harris said, clapping Colby on the back. "Let's mount up and ride over to the house."

"My mother wants us to stop by the big house before we leave," Billy said.

"We'll do just that," Mr. Harris said, leading the way on Big Red.

Colby waited to let Billy go next, and then he nudged Hank in the side with his heel and rode across the drive proudly.

Mrs. Sanchez came out on the back porch. She had a large picnic basket loaded with good things to eat. Colby grinned. He knew that Billy's mother had already packed everything she could think of to send with them. They wouldn't starve, that was for sure.

"You can have everything in here," Mrs. Sanchez said, smiling broadly. "I made fresh corn bread this morning. Fact is, it's still warm." She handed the basket to Mr. Harris and hurried back in the kitchen to return with another smaller basket.

"This one is for my man, Mr. Harris. Now you be sure he gets it."

"I'll hand it to him personally," Colby's father assured her.

Mrs. Sanchez came down the steps to put the basket in Mr. Harris' hands.

"I'll put it on the first horse, right behind Al, of course with hands-off orders," Mr. Harris said, smiling.

"Thank you," Mrs. Sanchez said. Then she went to Billy. Her son bent down to offer his cheek for her kiss.

"You be a good boy, Billy," she said, her eyes shining. "Don't cause Mr. Harris no trouble."

"I won't," Billy promised. He returned his mother's kiss.

"I want to say good-bye to my wife and boys," Mr. Harris told Al as the hand mounted his lead horse and picked up the rope to the pack horses.

"Well, I'll be on my way," Al said. "We'll meet you at the creek tonight."

As the horses slowly moved off down the lane, heading for the open range, Colby followed his father on horseback across the drive to say good-bye to his mother and brothers.

"The twins and I will miss you both," Mrs. Harris

said, first kissing her husband and then Colby. "We'll be praying for your safety."

Mr. Harris dismounted to kiss the twins and then got back in the saddle. He turned Big Red.

"Let's hit the trail!"

Colby called good-bye to the twins and his mother and waved as they passed the horse barns and were hidden from sight. He took a deep breath and let it out as Hank steadily plodded along behind Conchita and Big Red.

15
ON THE
TRAIL

Colby shifted wearily in his saddle. It was their second day on the trail. They had only been riding for about an hour since lunch, but already Colby was tired. He felt like he'd been sitting in the saddle forever.

He reached down and patted Hank on the shoulder. It was a beautiful day, just perfect for a trail ride. What his friends back in the city wouldn't give for a chance like this. Even Kevin had thought Colby was the luckiest guy around. Well, he was. Colby bit his bottom lip. He didn't like to think about Kevin.

Kevin was a good friend, but being around him reminded Colby that he still had not kept his promise to Kevin. Colby sighed. He had to find a way to talk with Billy about God.

"Look, boys!" Mr. Harris pointed toward the hills.

Billy and Colby both turned their heads to see what was happening. A herd of antelope raced gracefully across the range, startled by the presence of humans.

Colby stared in amazement. He had never seen anything so beautiful.

"Isn't that something?" Billy asked in awe.

Colby nodded. For a moment he had forgotten all about being tired of bouncing in the saddle, of riding. In fact, now he didn't feel half bad.

"Well, let's get going," Mr. Harris said. "We want to make the first camp by late afternoon."

Sometimes they let the horses canter or trot to break the monotony of the riding, but mostly the horses walked. The range went on and on, endlessly, and all of it was a part of the Two CC's Ranch.

As they rode higher in the plains, the air felt cooler, even though the sun was still shining brightly. Colby was glad he had his jacket strapped behind his saddle. At the next rest break, he untied it from the rawhide strings and put it on. He felt warmer right off.

"How much farther is it to the first line shack, Dad?" Colby asked as they loosened the cinches on the saddles to give the horses a rest.

"Oh, maybe another three miles. We'll get there before the sun goes down," Mr. Harris said, taking a drink from the canteen and passing it to the boys. "How are you two doing?"

"Just fine, Sir," Billy answered, grinning as he looked at Colby.

"All right, Dad," Colby added. He wasn't about to admit that his muscles were so tired and sore that he could hardly stand up. And to think that there were days and days of riding yet to come. Colby waited till his father sat down on the ground and then he dropped on his stomach beside him and rested his head on his arms. The next thing he knew, his father was shaking him.

"Time to go, Son," Mr. Harris said gently.

Colby sat up, his face growing red with embarrassment. Billy was already on Conchita, ready to ride. Quickly, Colby tightened the cinch on Hank and rebridled his horse. He had been trying to prove that he was as much a man as anybody else, and he'd blown it by falling asleep before the second full day's ride was over.

"That was a good rest," Mr. Harris said, nodding with satisfaction. "I needed a few winks myself. Let's move out."

Colby fell into line behind his father's horse with Billy in the rear. The sun was sliding behind the mountains when Mr. Harris pulled Big Red to a halt.

"There's the first line shack," he said, motioning ahead of them.

Colby strained his eyes to pick out the small log cabin nestled in the trees. It looked so peaceful—just like it belonged in the hills.

"Mac's dog ought to announce our visit any time now," Mr. Harris said as they started up the narrow trail to the cabin. Just as he spoke, a small black and white dog raced down the trail toward them, barking frantically.

The horses picked their way up the hill, finally coming into the cabin's small clearing.

"Welcome, welcome," Mac Loden greeted, coming out

to meet them. He was a big husky man with a full beard and lots of reddish hair.

"There's plenty of food in the cupboard," Mr. Loden said. "You get those horses taken care of, and I'll rustle us up a feast fit for a king."

With speed brought by practice, Billy and Colby unsaddled their horses and soon had them watered and hobbled in the grassy pasture near the cabin.

"Ummm, this fresh beef sure tastes good," Mac said as he bit into a thick steak sometime later. "I get a lot of game up here—rabbits, squirrels, and the like. But it's been a long time since I sank my teeth into a juicy steak."

"I guess you look forward to the supply train," Colby said.

Everyone laughed. Colby blushed.

"Yes, Son, you're right. I do look forward to the fresh food the fellows bring. But more than that, I look forward to the company. The nights get sort of lonely here sometimes."

"Are there bears up here?" Colby asked, his eyes wide. Just then, an owl hooted in the tree nearby. Colby jumped.

Mac Loden chuckled. "Been known to be some bears. Mostly it gets cold and miserable at night. Course I have Packy here for company." He reached beside him and patted the black and white Australian terrier by his side. "She's pretty good protection too, but a man needs someone to talk to once in a while."

"Sounds pretty lonely up here," Billy said.

Mac rubbed his chin thoughtfully. "Sometimes it is. But mostly it isn't. I have the cattle, my horse, Packy, my guitar, and my Bible—what more could a man want?"

Later that night Colby and Billy lay inside the cabin in hammocks hung from the ceiling, just for "company" Mac had said. Outside they could hear the melodic strumming of Mac's guitar and the soft mumbling of conversation between the two men.

"I think I'd like to live up here," Colby said. "I like the quiet, the wide open spaces, and the thought of being on my own."

"Me too," Billy agreed. He was silent a moment and then he spoke again. "I didn't know Mr. Loden very well at the ranch. He's pretty much always been a line shack hand. I didn't know he was sort of crazy about religion."

Colby swallowed so suddenly he almost choked. "Crazy? I don't think he's crazy," he said finally. "Just because a guy asks God's blessing on his food and reads the Bible—does that make him crazy? Mr. Loden believes there is a God who watches over him. It's the same way my dad and I believe."

"I know you go to church all the time, but do you really believe that God cares about you?"

Colby nodded in the dark. "I sure do. The Bible tells us that God even watches over the sparrows. Do you know that God knows how many hairs there are on your head?"

"You're kiddin'," Billy said.

"No, it's true," Colby insisted.

"How do you learn all that stuff?"

"I learn a lot at church," Colby told him. "And I used to go to a club for guys at the church where I came from. There we learned a lot about God. We had a lot of fun too." Colby took a deep breath. He felt kind of shaky now that he was finally talking to Billy about God.

"We're trying to build up our class at church so we can get together and have fun learning about God. We'd sure like you to come—Kevin and me, I mean. How about it?" He waited for Billy's answer. "Billy?" he said softly. *He must have fallen asleep while I was talking,* Colby thought. *Or had he?*

Colby closed his own eyes and listened to the soft music coming through the open windows.

16
END OF
THE LINE

There were cattle and more cattle and horses everywhere they went. The three riders rode for miles on end, never out of the sight of Two CC's stock. After the first few days, Colby no longer dreaded getting into the saddle and riding.

In five days, Colby had met Mac Loden, Jesse Wright, and Pete Hayden. Next they would come to the most remote shack of them all—the one manned by Billy's father, José Sanchez.

Colby could tell that Billy was anxious. He was up before anyone else and had the campfire burning brightly and the coffee heating. Mr. Harris had allowed the boys to drink coffee since the start of the ride.

"I bet you can hardly wait to see you dad," Colby said as they saddled up the horses to ride out.

Billy grinned and nodded.

"Think he'll remember you?" Colby teased.

"You'll see," was all Billy would say.

Toward noon they stopped to rest along the narrow creek that ran from the mountains to the canyon bottom.

"We should be there in another hour, Billy," Mr. Harris said as he loosened the cinch on Big Red and allowed the horse to graze on the tall tender grasses.

Billy grinned. His face showed his excitement, but his words were solemn. "Sure looks like a storm coming," he said, staring into the sky.

Colby followed Billy's gaze. Dark clouds were gathering over the mountains. The air was heavy and still.

"Anyone for a chocolate bar?" Mr. Harris reached into his pack and took out three crushed candy bars. The sun had melted and remelted them many times along the miles.

"Just about anything would taste good right now," Colby admitted, reaching for the soft chocolate. They ate two main meals a day, breakfast and supper, both around the campfire. Lunch was a rest stop where they munched on anything they could find. All the goodies Mrs. Sanchez had sent were long gone.

After a short rest, they were back in the saddle. The trail was leveling out now, approaching the plateau the cattle grazed on at the farthermost pasture of the Two CC's Ranch.

"Hey, look!" Billy shouted. "Mr. Harris, there's a cow and her new calf."

Both Colby and his father turned to look at the sturdy little red and white calf and its mother, nearly hidden by the thick brush.

"Go ahead, boys. See if you can flush them out," Mr. Harris said, nodding.

"Whooppee!" Billy shouted. He kicked Conchita into a canter and raced toward the cow.

Colby followed a little slower on Hank. He wasn't so sure just what he and Billy were supposed to do. Oh, he had seen the cowhands cut cattle at the ranch, but that was different. There was a corral there. This was wide-open range. Besides, it didn't look like the mother cow intended to budge from the thicket with her calf.

Just then the cow broke out of the brush and started to run away from Billy and Conchita. Without warning, Hank whirled on his heels and planted himself in front of the cow. Colby yelled and hung on for dear life. He had almost been whipped out of the saddle one more time. Frantically, he gripped the saddle horn with both hands, ignoring the loose reins which hung on Hank's neck.

After a few more sharp moves, Colby relaxed a bit and began to feel Hank's next move and go with the horse. When the cow and her calf were finally trotting toward the rest of the herd, nearly a mile away, Billy and Colby rode back to Mr. Harris.

"Dad, did you see what Hank did?" Colby asked breathlessly. "I've never done anything so neat in my life! He knows how to herd a cow all by himself."

Mr. Harris chuckled. "Riding a cuttin' horse is quite an experience, Son. I'm glad you stayed in the saddle."

Colby grinned sheepishly. "I almost didn't when Hank made that first turn. I never dreamed he could move that fast." He looked at Billy. "And you said my horse was a plug."

"Yeah," Billy smiled and wrinkled his nose in apology. "I figured I was pretty safe 'cause I knew nobody had bothered to tell you that Hank was champion cutting horse at the rodeo three years in a row, awhile back."

"Honest?" Colby glanced at his father.

"That's right, Son," Mr. Harris agreed. "Hank is one of the best cow horses in the country. Of course, he's a bit old and out of shape to do that all the time. But I reckon he could still keep up with the best of 'em."

Mr. Harris straightened up in the saddle and picked up the reins. "Well, let's get going. Less than a mile and we'll be at the line shack." He nodded to Billy who urged Conchita into the lead on the trail.

The one room line shack was in sight, nestled in among the huge pine trees when Billy reined Conchita to a halt. He waited till Mr. Harris and Colby rode up beside him.

"Something's wrong," Billy said, a worried frown on his forehead. "Solo should have been barking his head off by now. Solo is my father's dog," he explained. "They have been partners together at this line shack ever since Solo was a puppy."

Mr. Harris frowned. "Let's get moving." He urged Big Red into a trot and led the way up the path.

The door of the cabin was open and coals from the breakfast fire still smoldered in the fire pit outside. Mr. Harris swung out of the saddle and quickly tied Big Red to the hitching post that stood at one side of the clearing.

"Anybody here?" he called loudly.

"Dad? Dad? Are you here? I'll check the lean-to where Dad keeps his horse," Billy said, hurrying around the side of the cabin. In a moment he was back. "Poncho is hobbled right out back. Now I *know* something is wrong," Billy's voice quivered.

"Wait a minute! Listen!" Colby interrupted.

The three of them stood silently as the sound of a dog's barking echoed through the heavy air.

"Up there, in the trees," Billy shouted. He began running up the path which led into the woods behind the cabin.

"Come on, Son," Mr. Harris ordered.

Quickly, Colby tied Hank beside Conchita and Big Red and ran up the trail behind his father and Billy. His heart began to pound, both from the running and from the fear that something bad had happened. Colby rounded a curve in the path and saw his father and Billy kneeling up ahead. There was Mr. Sanchez sprawled on the ground beside a large log.

Colby struggled for his breath as he looked down at Billy's father. A lump filled his throat. How badly was Mr. Sanchez hurt?

"Tried ... tried to get out of the way of the tree," Mr. Sanchez said, motioning feebly toward a large tree lying almost on top of him. "Saw it falling wrong. When ... when I tried to move, I fell. Must have broke my leg." He stopped for breath. His pain was so great that he could barely talk.

"We've got to get you out of here," Mr. Harris said briskly. "Colby! Billy! Hand me your jackets and both of your belts. I'll need the straightest branches you can find. Billy, run to the cabin and bring me a blanket. Colby, we'll need two long poles to rig up a stretcher," Mr. Harris barked, as he gently explored the injured man's leg with his fingertips.

Colby looked at Billy. His friend's face was pale with worry. Colby took a deep breath and picked up the hatchet to cut some long poles.

Colby knew it hadn't taken very long, but it seemed like hours before they had built a stretcher. Mr. Harris used their jackets and belts with sticks to hold Mr. Sanchez's set leg in place for the trip back to the cabin.

Though they gently carried him in the stretcher, Mr Sanchez moaned with each move.

Finally, Mr. Sanchez was lying on the narrow cot at the back of the line shack.

"Is there anything I can do for you, Father?" Billy asked anxiously.

Mr. Sanchez shook his head. "I am grateful you came when you did. I was there on the ground no more than an hour or so, but it seemed like a very long time with my leg hurting so." He shuddered. "I do not like to think what might have happened if you had not come."

"I have to get help for you," Mr. Harris explained. "The rain will begin soon, and I'd like to be down the trail some when it comes. If I really push Big Red, I should be able to reach the next line shack within a few hours. I can get a fresh mount at each station. I should be back with a replacement for you in three days at the most."

Mr. Harris smiled. "By that time, you'll feel well enough for the trip out, and your wife's good care will have you up and around in no time once you're back at the ranch." He turned to the boys. "I'm leaving you two in charge. Mr. Sanchez will tell you what needs to be done. Make sure he gets plenty of rest. I'll be back as soon as I can."

"Everything will be fine," Mr. Sanchez said weakly.

Mr. Harris clasped Colby on the shoulder for a moment, then he was gone.

Colby listened to the sound of Big Red's galloping

hooves on the hard trail. A lonesome feeling came over him. Time and good care would heal Mr. Sanchez's broken leg. But what if something happened to his father as he rode the trail alone?

Colby turned from the doorway. *Please be with Dad, dear God,* he prayed silently. He looked back outside staring down the trail as the wind whipped the huge pine trees.

17 THE STORM

Colby sat and counted the cracks in the board floor. Mr. Sanchez had been asleep for several hours now. Billy hadn't left his father's side for a moment. Though there was no noise to disturb him, Mr. Sanchez sometimes moaned in his sleep from his painful broken leg.

It would be suppertime before long. They would have to eat something cold from the supply of cans on the cabin shelves. It was too windy to start a fire in the cooking pit outdoors.

Colby went to the door and looked at the sky. It was almost black in the west. The storm that had threatened since noon was finally coming. Colby sighed and turned back inside the cabin. He tried to move as quietly as possible so that he wouldn't wake up Mr. Sanchez.

"Would you like some water, Father?" Billy asked as his father stirred.

Colby walked over to the bed.

"Are you feeling better, Sir?" he asked.

Mr. Sanchez nodded. "My old leg sure hurts though," he said slowly.

"I'll rustle up some food, Dad," Billy said. "Think you can eat?"

"A broken leg don't hurt my appetite none, Son," Mr. Sanchez said, his voice sounding stronger.

"I'll help you," Colby offered.

Billy took a can of pork and beans from the shelf and hunted for a can opener. Just then a streak of lightning flashed, lighting up the whole cabin. In a few seconds, the three heard a rumble of thunder.

"It's sure going to rain," Colby commented as he took three plates and started toward the crude plank table.

No sooner were the words out of his mouth than the rain began. It beat against the thick cabin walls. Colby set the plates on the table and hurried to close the door against the pouring rain. He saw Mr. Sanchez struggling to sit up. The man's face was white with pain.

"You can't get up!" Colby cried.

"The cattle . . . in the canyon. There's near 30 cows . . . with calves." Mr. Sanchez forced the words out. "This kind of rain will cause . . . flooding." He dropped back against the pillow, exhausted from the pain.

"We'll have to do something," Billy said anxiously. "I've seen how fast the canyon creek can rise and overflow its banks with a heavy rain." He turned to his father. "We'll take care of it, Dad. I'll round up the cows and calves and get them up the plateau with the rest of the herd."

"No!" Colby took a deep breath. "You stay here with your dad. I'll go and round up the cows and calves. You just tell me where to find them."

"You can't do it," Billy said in dismay. "You don't know anything about herding cattle. It isn't as easy as it looks."

"I'm just a greenhorn, I know that," Colby said with a lot more confidence than he felt, "but Hank knows what to do. We'll get the job done. Your father needs you here."

With the rain beating against his poncho, Colby rode toward the canyon. He wasn't sure that he could do the job ahead of him—even with his championship cutting horse. Colby tipped his head so the water would run off his hat. Then he squinted against the rain to see the path.

The rocky trail led down, down, down into the lush green canyon. No wonder the cows preferred to graze here. As Colby rode along the creek bank, he could see that the water was already rising. If the rain kept up, it wouldn't be long before the water would overflow its banks.

Finally, Colby could see the dark outlines of several cows and their calves up ahead. The animals had their backs to the wind, heads down, and were doggedly trying to fend off the driving rain. Colby tried to forget about how cold he felt.

"OK, Boy," he said out loud to Hank. "We've got to get these cows and their babies out of the canyon to safety. Mr. Sanchez is depending on us."

Hank plodded along dejectedly, soaking wet from the cold sheets of rain. The cows didn't want to face into the driving rain and leave the canyon. Hank managed to keep his footing on the slippery ground. Colby, thankful that Hank knew what to do, held onto the saddle horn and allowed the horse to work.

Finally, there were 6 cows and their calves headed out toward the high land. Colby let them go and turned Hank back to head deeper into the canyon. Mr. Sanchez had said 30 cows and some calves were pasturing there. That meant that 24 animals were still scattered over the canyon floor.

Over and over, Colby and Hank ran into small groups of cows and sent them out of the canyon. When he was certain that there were no others, and he had counted 30 cows and their calves, Colby headed Hank toward the mouth of the canyon.

Soon he caught up with the slow-moving cattle. The cows plodded steadily along, mooing loudly for their babies to stay close. Near the end of the canyon, one stubborn old cow ran past Colby back into the canyon. Colby hesitated. Should he chase the cow and her calf and leave the rest of the animals, or should he let her go?

Colby decided he'd go back for the straggler and her calf later.

By the time the other cows were reunited with the main herd, Colby was shivering. His fingers were numb. He was so tired he could hardly sit in the saddle. What difference would it make if he left one cow and her calf in the canyon? The creek probably wouldn't flood too badly anyway.

Colby took a deep breath. He had promised to do his best. He shut his eyes for a long moment, feeling the rain on his cold face. "Dear God, help me, please."

Wearily, he opened his eyes and turned his tired horse back toward the canyon floor. The trail seemed twice as slippery as Hank picked his way back through the muddy rocks in the path. As he reached the creek, Colby opened his eyes in amazement. Just a short time ago, the creek had been a swiftly flowing stream—but now it was a raging river. The water gushed over its narrow banks, clutching at trees and shrubs in its way.

They would have to hurry. Colby urged Hank on, searching the brush and canyon sides for the missing cow and her calf. Colby spotted them at the far end of the canyon.

It took all of Hank's skills to budge the cow from the clump of brush where she had taken shelter. Finally, she and her calf headed out of the canyon again. But she was not convinced that she should leave. Mooing her anger, the old cow kept trying to turn and race past Hank back into the canyon.

At the mouth of the canyon, the cow gave one last bellow and trotted across to the rest of the herd as her calf followed. The job was done!

Hank stopped for a rest, his sides heaving. Colby slumped in the saddle. It took all his strength to pick up the reins and urge Hank back toward the shack.

When they reached the shack, Billy ran out and helped Colby out of his saddle. Billy led Colby inside and dressed him in warm, dry clothes. After that, Colby collapsed into his sleeping bag.

18
A
REWARD!

Colby turned over on the soft mattress, enjoying the cool smooth sheets against his skin. It seemed like forever since he had slept in a real bed. He'd forgotten how good it felt to sink down into the bed, covered with warm blankets.

Dan, Drew, and his mother had insisted on hearing about the entire trip, mile by mile, it seemed. Mr. Sanchez was going to be all right, thanks to Mr. Harris' skills at first aid and bone-setting.

Colby turned over as his stomach rumbled. His mother had immediately cooked a big dinner with mashed potatoes, steak, salad, and freshly baked bread with home-made butter. Colby sighed happily. He knew he was tired enough to fall asleep, but his mind wouldn't let him.

The twins had been excited with the pine cones he brought them. Billy's mother had promised to help them make cone people, just like she had done as a little girl in Mexico.

"Colby? Are you still awake?" his mother called up the stairs.

"Sure, Mom," he answered. *What could she want this late?*

"Could you slip into your clothes and come back downstairs?" she requested.

"Be right there," he said, throwing back the sheet and jumping out of bed.

"What's up?" he asked, coming into the kitchen. Mr. Claypool was sitting at the table with his father and mother.

"Have a seat, Son," his father said, nodding toward an empty chair. "Billy will be along shortly."

"Is something wrong?" Colby asked.

Before anyone could answer, Billy opened the back door. He hesitated at the sight of Mr. Claypool and then came into the kitchen slowly.

"Take a chair, Billy," Mr. Harris said, smiling. "The boss has something he wants to say to you boys."

Mr. Claypool pushed back his chair and rose to his feet. He walked a few steps away from the table and then turned around.

"I'm not much on fancy words, but you two boys did this spread proud with your work up on that line shack." Mr. Claypool cleared his throat. "Colby, you did the work of a top hand, bringin' those cattle and calves up out of that flooding canyon. Thirty head of cattle with young'ns ain't something to be sneezed at. And you, Billy, the way you kept care of your dad and both you boys kept things in line till relief came. Well . . . that was man's work too."

Colby looked at his dad. His father nodded his head in agreement. Colby felt his stomach churn excitedly.

The ranch owner cleared his throat. "We like to show folks we appreciate 'em on the Two CC's," Mr. Claypool went on. "I just happened by the foal barn the other day. The twins, Dan and Drew, were there, and they told me how you and Billy have taken to those look-alike colts. Now, I already figured that they were special colts, being twins and all."

Mr. Claypool looked at Billy and then at Colby. "I want each of you boys to have a colt," he said abruptly. "You can work out which one belongs to whom. By the time those babies are old enough to be trained, I reckon you boys will be smart enough and strong enough to handle that too."

He glanced knowingly at Mr. Harris. "From what I hear, you two fellows seem to be able to handle just about anything that goes on around here."

Colby swallowed and glanced at Billy. Did Mr. Claypool know about Billy's trouble with his son?

Mr. Claypool held out his hand to shake with each of the boys. "I'm just tryin' to say thanks."

"Wow!" Colby breathed.

"Thank you a lot, Sir," Billy said in one breath.

"Me too," Colby added. "I mean, thank you for the colt."

"You're welcome," the boss of the Two CC's said. He

nodded quickly to Colby's parents and walked out of the house.

"Yippee!" Billy shouted, jumping up and knocking the chair over backward.

"I don't believe it!" Colby shouted. He and Billy pounded each other happily.

"I can't wait to tell my dad!" Billy exclaimed. "Me, Billy Sanchez, with a horse all my own!"

"How about some milk and cookies to celebrate?" Mrs. Harris suggested.

"Sounds great, Mom," Colby said. "Hey . . wait a minute!"

"The colts!" Billy and Colby both shouted. Together, they headed for the door.

"Oh, you don't want to be running outside this late at night," Mrs. Harris protested.

"Now, Mother," Mr. Harris disagreed. "As new owners, the boys *should* check over their possessions. It'll just take a minute to slip out to the foal barn."

"I suppose," Mrs. Harris said with a sigh, but she was smiling.

The summer night was full of stars as Billy and Colby ran barefooted across the gravel drive to the dark barn. Colby took a deep breath of the warm night air. Except for the heat, it was just like being back in the mountains.

"I'll get the light," Billy said as they pulled open the heavy door.

The boys blinked at the brightness as they leaned across the stall door.

"You can have your pick first," Colby offered as they looked fondly down at the small brown colts resting on the clean straw.

"No, you choose the one you want first," Billy said.

Both boys laughed.

"We can decide that tomorrow," Colby said.

"And you know what?" Billy asked, suddenly serious. "We've got to start practicing for the rodeo. I almost forgot about it. We've only got a month at the most. It's held right after school starts. We can be in the boot race, the pig scramble, and the goat tying. My dad was pretty good at that when he was a kid. Now that he's here at the ranch, maybe he can help us learn how."

"Oh wow!" Colby exclaimed. Then he grinned. "Well, my dad is always saying that there is never a dull moment on a ranch."

"How could there be with you and me around?" Billy asked, grinning.

"I'll race you to the big house," Colby challenged.

"You're on," Billy shouted.

Colby flipped the light switch off. They paused long enough to close the door to the foal barn and then they were off, bare feet flying over the gravel stone drive, the faint breeze in their faces.

Suddenly, Billy stopped.

Colby halted and turned toward his friend.

"Hey," Billy said, breathing hard. "Is that offer to go to Sunday School still open?"

"You mean you'll go with me?" Colby asked, gasping for air. "Sure, I mean, of course I want you to go with me," he said, a bit confused.

"Okay, I'll go next Sunday," Billy said; then he took off in the lead toward the big ranch house.

Colby stared at him. Billy really wanted to go to church with him. God *was* answering his prayers. He grinned. It might not seem like much, but it was a beginning.